Queen of Tentacles

Bethany Browning

Also by Bethany Browning

When tarot card reader Carrie Dettwiler stumbles across the mayor's dead body on a random Tuesday, town gossip reaches a fever pitch—and everyone's convinced she and her rescue raven Waggery have performed a deadly dark ritual. Carrie deals with the cards she's been dealt, only to be blown off course by her gale-force feelings for tattoo artist Stormy Portwood, who breezes into town at the same time people start dying. Buy now.

"My god, this ticks so many boxes for me. All my favorite cozy tropes, a cool and clever love interest with a shadowy history, lots of tarot, an impressive amount of wordplay, and a scene-stealing talking raven who

SASQUATCH, BABY! IS THE WINNER OF THE 2023 BEST INDEPENDENT BOOK AWARD! After her posh Napa Valley friends cut her off for committing an unspeakable betrayal, Tabitha Eggs retreats to the redwood forests of Del Norte County, California, to drink herself to death. But when she stumbles over two decomposing corpses near her new home, she believes that walking into a wildfire is preferable to whatever waits in the woods. Her plans are foiled when she's kept alive by a curious Sasquatch, and they create a bizarre and everlasting union. Buy now.

After a bizarre accident leaves her motherless, Amy Jay escapes her violent stepfather and is taken under the wing of a small-town doctor. When the doctor's niece, a self-described mer-witch, arrives with potions, spells, mermaid tails, wigs, and costume jewelry, Amy Jay dives headfirst into the world of professional mermaiding. She gets a tail, a mer-name, an instruction book by a mysterious, missing mermaid—and still, something about her new life doesn't add up. But before Amy Jay can sort out what feels fishy, her stepfather locates her hideout and changes the course of her life forever. Buy now.

For Dante and Tazio. May your lives be filled with exciting mysteries, wild adventures, friendly pirates, and seafood stew when you need it.

Chapter One

I spun around and shot Stormy a killer look.

She picked up her phone and pretended to speak into it. "I'd like to report a murder. Sure, I'll hold."

"Stormy, stop it." I took another peek in the full-length mirror, turning this way and that to check every angle. I looked cute. Didn't I?

"Yes, hi," she continued without breaking eye contact with me. "The murder took place a few minutes ago at One Shanty Lane in Mariner's Cove. That's right. In the loft above Think Ink Tattoo. Did I see it myself? Sure did. Unspeakable carnage."

"It's a good look," I said, smoothing the wrinkles out of the T-shirt I'd sneaked out of her closet.

"Excuse me?" She held up a finger to shush me. "Who was murdered? It's less of a *who* and more of a *what*. It's fashion. Fashion is dead. My girlfriend killed it."

"Had your laugh?" I asked as I took a final glance at my bum. "I'm trying to fit in with your Mariner's Cove buddies."

I twirled.

She pretended to hang up the phone. "I called the fashion police. They'll be here directly."

"You have the number for the fashion police?" I asked.

"I do, and it's a good thing. What you're wearing," she gestured broadly in my direction, "is a sartorial crime."

"Stop it, Stormy," I said. "I'm already nervous enough."

"Be yourself," she said, taking me into her arms. "The Carrie I fell in love with would never wear leather leggings, boots, and a tee with a glitter skull on it."

"I thought—"

"Don't get me wrong, it's a bangin' outfit when I wear it. And," she gripped my bottom with both hands. "I like how it feels. But it looks like you're dressing up like me for Halloween."

"I don't—"

"Nope. I won't hear it," she said. "My Carrie wears cotton dresses and Mary Janes and a tatty old jean jacket torn up by her pet raven's claws. And she looks so beautiful my heart breaks in half at the thought of her."

"Stormy—"

She kissed me lightly and pulled me close.

Waggery, my raven, wolf-whistled from his perch.

"You're lovely, Carrie. You're sweetness, light, and sunshine. Now go change into something I'll look forward to getting you out of later."

I knew Stormy loved me as I was, but I appreciated the affirmation. Especially because I was about to make my debut as the in-house tarot card reader at Stormy's tattoo shop, Think Ink.

Two minutes later, I emerged from her bedroom in a peasant blouse, skater skirt, ribbed tights, and the well-worn Mary Janes. "Better?"

"There's my girl," she said. "Grab your cards and your murder bird and let's go blow the roof off Mariner's Cove with its first readings."

* * *

When Stormy Portwood and I first met, she swooned over the coziness of my cottage in Prosperity and claimed her home in Mariner's Cove was gloomy and drab by comparison.

She undersold it.

The spaces she occupied were large, comically so, for a single person. Stormy failed to mention the polished wood floors, exposed brick walls, the two fireplaces and—in the shop—an expansive wall painted deep black and highlighted with designs, tattoo prices, and artistic flourishes in thick, white paint. The Think Ink logo dominated the space, with quotes from famous philosophers, writers, and scientists in each fold of a gigantic brain.

"The brain gives people a spot to focus on when they're in the chair," she said. "They might learn something."

Think Ink was so gorgeous, passersby dropped in to gawk and walked out with a mark they would carry for the rest of their lives. That's the effect Stormy had on people.

Indelible.

Waggery and I had arrived in the morning, spirited through the winding roads in a sensible sedan loaned to me by my Uncle Grist. He didn't need it while he was honeymooning with his wife, Lillian, in Europe. Nothing was keeping me home in Prosperity either, so Stormy and I thought it would be fun for me to take up residence in Mariner's Cove for a while.

Situated on a rocky bluff that was equal parts awe-inspiring and terrifying, Mariner's Cove was a historic destination for smugglers, pirates, trappers, and thieves. It was an unapologetically rugged locale with heart-stirring views and heart-stopping surf in equal measure. In sharp contrast to Prosperity's bright, warm days, colorful native flowers, and breezy afternoons,

Mariner's Cove was all dense fog, craggy boulders, chilling sea spray, and, as it turned out, dark secrets.

The drive from Prosperity would have been spectacular if not for Waggery's carsickness. I spent half the time trying to keep my eyes on the winding road, and the other half peering into his crate to make sure he wasn't dying.

"Quok," Waggery uttered, a little too soft for my liking as I relocated him onto the perch Stormy had set up near the reading table in her tattoo shop.

"I think he's hungry," Stormy said. "When can he eat again?"

"Soon," I said. "I want to give it more time. Besides, all you have in the shop are Flamin' Hot Cheetos."

"I refuse to apologize for my food choices," Stormy said. "I am who I am and who I am is powered by Cheetos."

"No judgment here," I said. "Don't come crying to me when you're diagnosed with cheese dust disease."

"Oh, no! Oh, no!" Waggery cried before gacking onto the floor in front of his perch.

"Sorry, Stormy." I reached for a rag and spray cleaner behind the register.

Just then, the door blasted open, and a large shadow loomed over the shop.

I swear the temperature dropped twenty degrees.

Before me stood the largest man I'd ever seen in my life. Nearly seven feet tall. Bald. Ink covering almost every inch I could see, save for his face, which looked like it was chiseled out of granite.

Behind him, a group of what I could only assume were henchmen leered.

"Oh, no," Waggery called before he threw up on the floor. Again.

Queen of Tentacles

"I hope you've got a will, Stormy Portwood," the big man said. "You're about to die."

Chapter Two

The gang swarmed Think Ink and pulled weapons.

I tucked a wiggling Waggery under my arm, kicked over my reading table, and ducked behind it for cover. My cards went flying.

Stormy dove behind the checkout counter. She pulled her own weapon and pointed it at the ringleader.

"Not today," she said. "Never!"

"Eat lead, Portwood," the behemoth said with a sneer best described as 'dastardly'.

I heard clicking, as if they were all pulling triggers. I poked my head over the edge of the table to see Stormy speckled with red lights and pretending to die.

She collapsed and twitched on the floor.

Waggery pulled at my hair.

"It's okay," I said, petting him softly on the head.

"Well, blow me down! If we didn't take down a category five Stormy." The large man thudded his chest.

"Huzzah!" someone shouted, and a few others joined in with their own cheers—or were they jeers?

Stormy got up and brushed herself off.

"It's safe to come out now, Carrie," she said. "These dummies can't hurt you."

I stood up but continued to hold Waggery close. The last thing I needed was for him to be more stressed than he was.

"What in the actual hell?" I asked. "I thought we were all going to die in a hail of bullets. My heart is about to burst of out my chest. Are you okay, Stormy?"

"Carrie," said Stormy, pointing at the big guy, "I'd like you to meet Titanic Jones. And this is his band of pirates."

They all took a bow, except for the skinny one, who curtsied.

"It's a game, Carrie, and a stupid one. It's called Assassin, and all we do is hunt each other with fake weapons."

"I don't get it. How does it work?"

"We all have laser guns that look kind of real, and we stalk each other. I 'killed' them all last round by getting to their houses first thing in the morning and blasting them as they left for work. Busting in like this and blowing me away in front of my girlfriend is poor sportsmanship, if you ask me."

"All's fair in love and Assassin. You must be Carrie." Titanic's face broke into a broad smile. "We came by to welcome you, make you feel at home. Stormy's fake murder was icing on the cake."

He extended a hand the size of a baseball mitt.

"It's lovely to meet you, Milady," he said with a tiny, formal bow. "You're every bit as stunning as Stormy described. And Waggery! Wow! You weren't kidding, Stormy, he's an impressive bloke."

Waggery bowed his head and allowed Titanic to touch him gently on his beak.

"And this," he said, motioning to the ragtag scrum of tattooed, muscular men who had just fired fake weapons at my girlfriend, "is my band of Mariner's Cove marauders."

Titanic launched into introductions, bringing pirates by, one by one, to 'pay their respects,' as he put it. I met Seaweed McGee, Landlubber Lewis, Spyglass Steve, Shiver Me Kimber, Scurvy Doug, Diving Bill, Yo-ho Joe, and too many more to remember.

"You look like pirates, but are you actual pirates? Booty-stealing, treasure-hunting, ship-raiding pirates?"

"Arrrgghh," Waggery said, clearly remembering the time we went to a Halloween party as a dead buccaneer and her ghost parrot. He flew to his perch, and I was relieved he seemed to be feeling better.

Titanic let out a hearty laugh. "'*Aargh*' is right, my brother. Though we look like pirates, dress like pirates, and talk like pirates, we're the opposite of pirates."

"Yeah, they don't raid ships; they return things to ships," Stormy said, the smile on her face letting me know she was loving every minute of this.

Titanic handed me a business card. It read:

Preservation Pirates: Protecting Hidden Treasures
A 501 (c)(3) non-profit corporation

"What is this?" I asked.

"We look like rowdies, but we run a non-profit. We raise money to fund the protection of The Shipwrecks."

"The Shipwrecks?"

"I'll take you out there soon," Stormy said. "Five wrecked ships leaning against each other, all lined up on the beach. Titanic provides security and upkeep to keep vandals and looters from destroying them."

"Why have I not heard of The Shipwrecks?"

I thought of my history-obsessed Uncle Grist, who would never have been able to keep a beach brimming with shipwrecks a secret from me. If this was real, Grist would know.

"It's how we want it, Guppy," Titanic said. "You're not going to find The Shipwrecks in your Yelp reviews. Our life's work is keeping information about this historical marvel a secret. Even from history buffs."

"I'll believe it when I see it," I said.

"Challenge accepted," Stormy said. "I know the way. I drew the map."

"Aye, but she'll have to kill you after." Titanic leaned in and grimaced.

"Shiver me timbers," I said.

Titanic's laughter boomed out of him like a cannon. Waggery leaped above his perch and flapped his wings.

"Let's get the party started, Stormy," he said. "We'll show Carrie how we do things in Mariner's Cove."

"I told you I hung out with pirates," she said with a shrug.

"Stormy here is an honorary member," Titanic said. "We help her out with upgrades to her building in exchange for the best ink on the West Coast."

"Enough shop talk," Stormy yelled. She clapped her hands together. "Titanic! Cocktails!"

The next few hours passed in a blur of dark rum, homemade mead, and sea shanties (with varying degrees of offensive lyrics), tarot card readings, and tattoos for everyone.

They were a friendly and chatty group. I found out Seaweed McGee had a sweetie in the Sierras whom he hadn't seen in several weeks because she's on a Sasquatch-hunting expedition. Shiver Me Kimber was writing a romance novel, and Yo-ho Joe was a competitive ballroom dancer.

I was impressed by their many talents and their gentlemanly behavior, despite the fact that they'd burst in on a murderous manhunt.

Scurvy Doug cleaned up the bird vomit I'd forgotten about. He also appeared to be getting drunk, fast.

Before I could cross the room to get Scurvy Doug a glass of water, Diving Bill sat down at my table. He flipped the script and offered to read my cards for me.

"What is your question, Scalawag?" he asked as he shuffled.

You'll forgive me for not remembering the exact phrasing, but my question went something like this: "How the happy will I be here when staying here in my Stormy's Mariner's Cove?"

"Enjoying a bit of word salad, I see," Diving Bill said, shuffling and smiling. "Let's discover what the cards portend for you today."

Why were there two of him?

"Are you twins?" I asked.

I couldn't remember the last time I day drank.

I couldn't remember my name.

"Focus, Carrie," he said. "Pull your cards."

"Oh, right."

The first was the Eight of Cups, which depicts a red-cloaked figure walking away on a rocky beach.

"This is baaaaad," I said, sobering ever so slightly.

"Why?" Diving Bill asked.

"This person? She's walking away from a bitterly disappointing situation. She's given up. She's taking her walking stick and going home." I blew a raspberry. "Booo! Bad card."

Waggery blew a raspberry in solidarity.

"To me, she looks like a lady out for a nice walk. To The Shipwrecks, perhaps? Let's pull another one," he said.

"Yes. Pull another one, Matey."

"As you wish."

The Nine of Swords shows a woman in bed, in despair. "This means terror. Nightmares. Desperation," I said. "Yikes."

This was a negative read. Under normal circumstances with

a client, I'd stop turning cards and move the proceedings into Aunt Inez's garden to talk through what was going on. When the energy feels ugly, I offer a reset. Pulling another negative card can cause unnecessary pain, and I never want to cause bad feelings in a reading.

I didn't take my own advice.

"One more," I said. "Third time's the charm."

"Okay," he said and placed another card in front of me.

It was The Devil, reversed.

"He looks like a sinister guy," he said. "What does this card mean?"

"It's not as bad as it looks, but it's not great," I said. "Ugh, it means I'm trapped."

I pushed the cards away.

"It's a good thing tarot is all made-up nonsense," Diving Bill said.

"Say that again, and you'll find yourself in Davy Jones's Locker."

"You believe in all this psychic mumbo-jumbo?" he asked.

"I'm not a psychic," I said. "I'm a highly trained card reader. Learned from my Aunt Inez, who was the best. It's no more made-up nonsense than your pirate schtick."

He laughed. "Oh well, the pirate stuff is completely made-up. I help this band of miscreants on the weekends, but my full-time job is coroner."

"Coroner? You look at dead people all day?"

"Not all day," he said, stifling a laugh. "How many people do you think die in Mariner's Cove? Not so many. It's one of the few remaining burgs in California where the coroner is permitted to do autopsies."

"I did not know this information," I said. "Interesting."

"I'm also an accomplished knitter. See the scarf Titanic is wearing?"

"No!" I said, squinting my eyes in a weak attempt to focus on the fetching red and blue scarf around Titanic's neck. It was so large; on any other person it would have been a shawl. "You made it? It's pretty. You are *soo talertend*."

"And this sweater," he said, patting his chest. "And every beanie on every pirate in this room."

"That's a lot of beanies," I said. "It's a rainbow of beanies in here."

"I'll knit for you if you'd like. Gloves. Scarf, maybe?"

"I would *knot* say no," I said.

"Ha! You made a pun."

"All joking aside," I said. "I'd love a knitted thing. This place is colder than Bluebeard's basement."

"I do a few other things, too," he said.

"Like what?"

He leaned in real close. "If I told you, I'd have to kill you."

"Tell me," I said.

He broke into a big smile. "Obviously, I'm joking, Carrie. Everyone in this room has gigs, side gigs, main gigs...You have a real job to earn money in addition to tarot readings, don't you?"

"Oh, shut up," I said, taking a long swig of something rummy.

* * *

My grumpy mood didn't stick. It was nothing a few more drams of Seaweed McGee's homemade mead couldn't cure. I may have danced on my tarot card table. I shared a fish sandwich with Waggery, kindly provided by Titanic after I fell out of my chair, and he realized a small woman should have some protein when drinking rum at three in the afternoon.

"*Arrrgh*," Waggery said, loving it.

Stormy, done with her tattoos for the day, was working to

catch up with the rest of us. She fed Waggery some more for me because, apparently, I wasn't interested in anything but singing a song about heaving and hoeing and rolling and going with a guy named Randy.

The sun began to set. The evening wind howled and chilly puffs of sea air breached the wooden window frames. Stormy gave me her jacket.

"You've got to start bringing warmer clothes to Mariner's Cove," she said. "Or better yet, maybe you can leave them here."

"Diving Bill is a scarf making for me," I said. "I love him. He's my most, best friend."

"What?"

"This is the greatest day of my whole life," I said.

"This?" She nuzzled my neck. "You wait. We're just getting started."

§

"Tarot's no party trick, Carrie, and you shouldn't treat it as such."

I'd been kicked out of Daisy's seventh-grade slumber party for 'summoning Satan', as her mother put it. I wasn't sure why Aunt Inez was scolding me. I'd already been punished.

Waggery, perched on her shoulder, blew a raspberry.

"Can we go home now? You showed up looking like you swept in on a broom. Pun intended. Not helpful."

She glanced down at her moon-and-stars caftan. She was quiet as we walked.

The silence was a too-tight jacket. "I think it was a setup. They wanted a reason to kick me out. To make fun of me."

"Classic slumber party cruelty," she said. "Should be banned as hazing rituals."

My throat tightened. "I thought they wanted to be friends."

"Those girls? They don't have what you have. They're jealous."

I didn't see any reason why anyone would be jealous of me. "My parents are dead. They think I'm a witch." There was so much more I wasn't ready to tell her. I understood Inez was sticking up for me, but the truth still stung. The girls had invited me to alienate me.

"Why don't we call your friend Hank? It's still early enough for a movie. Grist can make popcorn."

"Nah," I said. "Hank and I are hanging out tomorrow."

Waggery giggled. Inez put her arm around my shoulder.

"You don't see it now, Carrie," she said. "One day, you'll find your people. There's a huge world full of witches, wizards, pirates, giants, and fortune tellers. And they're going to be crazy about you."

§

Chapter Three

Being the second drunkest person in the room (behind Scurvy Doug) and wanting the party to go all night long doesn't mean your fellow partiers are ready to make the same commitment.

"Keep singing those sea shanties, Carrie," Stormy said. "We'll clean everything up."

"I'll swab the decks!" I said, barely able to lift my head off the table.

I did not swab the decks.

Titanic and his band of looters efficiently cleaned up glassware, tidied up plates and napkins, wiped surfaces, and ran full bags of trash out to the bins behind the shop.

I was busy trying to remember if Sally Brown liked the scrumpy or the rumpy-pumpy—or both—when the door blew open for the last time.

The room fell silent.

"How dare you!"

A woman wrapped in an array of multicolored scarves walked slowly in my direction. She pointed a craggy, jewel-encrusted finger.

"You try to stake a claim on Baba Caracatiţă's territory?"

She smelled of sandalwood incense. I stood up. The room was a tilt-a-whirl.

"There is only room for one fortune teller in Mariner's Cove!" she shrieked. "You must leave at once! You are not safe here, Carrie Dettwiler."

"Not to worry," I said, thumping my temple with my index finger. "I'm a tarot card reader. Not a fortune teller."

I gave her a thumbs up.

"Do you take a mocking tone with me?"

Waggery growled and flew to my shoulder.

He was heavier than usual.

I was heavier than usual.

"You dare threaten me with your familiar!"

"This is Waggery," I said. "Not a familiar. And I'm not a fortune teller. Say it with me, *taare-ohhh*. Wait, how do you know my name?"

"Now wait a minute, Ms. Baba," Titanic stepped toward us. "There's been a misunderstanding."

"Hold your line!" Baba yelled. "Don't come any closer."

"Ms. Baba, is it? I'm Stormy. This is Carrie, but you knew that somehow. And you've met Waggery. Carrie is only here for a short time and only reading tarot cards. I am sure you'll find you both—"

"This interloper must pack up her things and leave town, never to return, or there will be hell to pay."

"Hold on there, Hot Pants," I said. "You will not threaten me. I have never interpolled anyone. I have an Engrish demgree from Starnford."

Baba Caracatiţă shaped her fingers in the form of a claw and walked toward me making hissing sounds.

"Is this for real?" I said, looking around to see if anyone else was seeing this or if I'd already passed out. "Are you hexing me?"

"It's Baba's curse," she said. "Leave town, or you'll pay."

Everyone ducked as if she was spraying hot oil around the room.

Waggery launched off my shoulder and flew toward her, flapping his wings. Baba swatted at him.

"Do. Not. Hurt. My. Bird," I said in a voice I did not recognize. "You get out of here right now or I will curse you, you hateful hag."

The gasp from the crowd was theatrical.

"Call off your minion!" Baba cried as Waggery landed on her shoulder. She leaned in and lowered her voice. Her eyes were crystal blue. She smelled like cinnamon. "Carrie, you must leave. There is danger."

"Waggery, come here. Now."

He flew back to me, but not before he barfed all over Baba's very silky—and expensive-looking—scarves.

Scurvy Doug shouted something about murder, fell off his chair, and crumpled in a heap on the floor.

"You poison me with dark magic emitted forth from this foul hell bird!"

Baba stripped off her slimed scarves.

She seemed to be enjoying her performance a little too much. She was trying to scare me.

But her eardrum-piercing voice and scenery-chewing performance weren't what got my attention. What frightened me was when she got quiet.

"You listen to me," she said, leaning in real close. "I'll unleash the power of my ancestors if I ever see you in Mariner's Cove again. You take your little friend and go back to where you belong. The hex is real. It's real, Carrie. You need to go."

Fueled by rum and mead, and not wanting to look like a

wimp in front of my new pirate friends, I matched her sinister tone and took a step toward her.

"Oh, you want to play magic games?" I asked. "How's this for a hex? You come near me again and I will make you walk the plank, old lady. No magic needed. Just a two-by-four, the briny sea, and a shove. Come at me and find out what I'm capable of. Aaargh!"

Baba grabbed my hand. "Where did you get this?" she asked, eyeing my emerald ring. It had been given to me from beyond the grave by Aunt Inez, and Stormy had an identical one. Stormy and I were soulmates, and we believed these rings proved it—even if we didn't know why or how yet.

Scurvy Doug somehow scraped himself off the floor long enough to run toward Baba. He lunged. The rest of the pirates dove in to pull him off, and I stood back and watched the melee.

"Ooookayyy," Stormy said, her voice shaking. "Enough. Baba, I'm going to have to ask you to leave. Carrie and Scurvy Doug, I'm going to have to ask you to both to sober up."

Baba was disheveled, but she appeared unharmed.

"We hear you, Baba, and I hope we can work this out," Stormy said. "Tensions are high, drinks have been flowing and—"

And, in a breath, Baba disappeared.

Stormy's face was ashen. Titanic looked like he'd seen a kraken. Scurvy Doug was passed out in the corner. And Diving Bill cut a wide berth around me, avoiding eye contact, as he scurried out the door—no doubt hoping to avoid getting wrapped up in a scuffle that could damage his professional reputation.

"She seemed nice," I said.

"She fired across your bow, lass," Titanic said. "You're going to need to parley."

"English, please," I said.

"Go smooth it over. She's threatened by you," Titanic said. "Make nice. Tell her you won't steal her clients."

"Right," Stormy said. "Go see her tomorrow. You're three sheets to the wind, Seadog. Sleep it off." She pointed toward the stairs.

"Aye, aye, Cappin'." I saluted the stunned crowd as I slowly made my way up the stairs, Waggery hopping alongside me, right by my feet, like the excellent familiar he was.

Chapter Four

"I did what now?"

The next morning began exactly as I deserved. Skull-crushing headache. Dry mouth. Classic hangover.

I also had an irritated, fussy raven who was ready for a walk and refused to let me sleep.

He also needed breakfast, so I shuffled into the kitchen and made him a plate of fruit and almonds. Stormy told me everything she saw me do, plowing through the story with increasing theatrics as I sank deeper and deeper into my embarrassment.

"I didn't think you had it in you, Dettwiler," she said, chuckling. "I loved it, personally. '*I'll make you walk the plank.*' Hilarious."

"I need to apologize to Baba," I said. "I can't have an old woman thinking I actually want to send her to Davy Crockett's basket."

"Jones," Stormy said. "Locker."

"What?"

"It's Davy Jones's locker. You had all the pirate lingo down like a pro last night."

I was still in my clothes from yesterday. "I'm going to go to her house right now."

"I don't know, Carrie," Stormy said. "I think you should let things cool off."

"Titanic said I needed to parsley."

"Parley. And Titanic is nearly seven feet tall," she said. "Everyone's afraid of him."

"It's the right thing to do. I said terrible things. She believes I'm an existential threat to her livelihood. Plus, Waggery needs a walk."

"Carrie, I—"

"You can't stop me."

"Where does she live?"

"I won't stop you," she said, backing up. "But unless you want her to drop dead from the smell, I'd highly recommend you take a shower and brush your teeth first."

* * *

Waggery was elated to be on a walkabout in Mariner's Cove. He puffed his feathers and made a few purring noises. He had good reason to feel happy. Mariner's Cove was filled with ravens—sea ravens—who were sturdier, tougher, and bolder than the Prosperity ravens. I'm no expert, but from what I could tell, ravens who lived by the sea were a deeper black with thicker feathers, possibly owing to the steady diet of fish and sea kelp combined with the near-constant buffeting by marine winds. They had beefier bodies.

He stayed close, never flying more than a few feet in front of me, but I could tell that he . They circled overhead, looping and diving. I wondered if they were curious about why he was accompanied by a human companion.

I amused myself by imagining their thoughts. Did they see Waggery as a traitor? A genius? Both? Neither?

"Looks like fun, doesn't it, Waggery? Doing loop-de-loops in the wind?"

He was uncharacteristically silent while observing these strange versions of himself.

"Don't go feral on me," I said. "I'd miss you too much to lose you to a conspiracy of sea ravens, as exciting as they are. I know what it's like, though. I almost joined a band of pirates last night. Let's make a deal. You stay near me, always, and I won't stow away on a sloop to Treasure Island or whatever."

He took my words literally and settled on my shoulder. At home in Prosperity, where he feels like he owns the place, the risk of him refusing to come out of a tree or down from someone's roof when I was running late was very high. Here, he seemed awestruck, humbled. Frankly, it made for a pleasant outing, and it gave me a peaceful moment to try to decipher the map of Mariner's Cove Stormy had given me. 'X' marked the spot where Stormy thought Baba's house was, gleaned from Baba's web page.

"Since you're a pirate now, your maps should all have X's marking the treasure," Stormy said just to be funny. As much as I appreciated her artistic abilities, I could have done with more street names and fewer flourishes, like dragons coming out of the sea and curlicues to represent the fog.

I could have waited for Stormy to finish her appointments, I suppose, but the last thing I needed was Baba being angry and plotting against me for another day. Besides, I didn't want to risk being a burden to Stormy or expect her to clean up my messes.

"This was my mistake," I said out loud, "so I should be the one to fix it."

The sidewalk ended and the rest of the way to Baba's

traversed a scraggly footpath that ascended a hill and disappeared into a stand of redwood trees.

"Looks like we're going hiking," I said to Waggery, who was resolute and serious on my shoulder as we took our first steps onto the path.

The climb was anything but effortless, and as I huffed and puffed and broke into a rum-scented sweat, I became quite curious about how a woman of Baba's advanced age made her way up and down the hill every day.

"She must have thighs of steel," I muttered to no one as I hoisted myself over a rocky outcropping.

The breeze picked up, rustled the leaves on the trees, and sent puffs of fog swirling around the top of the hill. As I took in the dramatic shifts and sways of the foliage, I saw something else, something human, duck behind a tree.

It was a woman. Long red hair trailed from the hood of her gray cloak. She darted through the trees in the forest and vanished.

She was probably one of Baba's clients on her way to an appointment. People sneaking in and out of appointments was common in my line of work. I had a handful of clients who parked far away and then entered through the garden door so their friends and co-workers wouldn't catch them visiting the crazy tarot reader. It used to hurt my feelings, but I got over it when I realized their money was as good as anyone's. Like most people, I had bills to pay.

The path was twistier and narrower once I was inside the forest. The light was dimmer, and the trail was flat. I took a deep breath; the air was so clean. A small bridge crossed over a happily burbling creek; a spotted towhee and a dark-eyed junco flitted in and out of the underbrush. Impossibly lush and thick ferns were almost neon green despite the gloomy darkness.

One more curve in the path and I was face-to-face with a

witch's cottage lifted straight from the imaginations of the Brothers Grimm.

The house appeared to be built directly into the side of a low cliff, with a barely visible roof tucked into an ominous over-hang that could crush the entire structure if it fell. Thick forest engulfed the top of the cliff, and I couldn't see how deep it was or to where it led. If you opened Baba's front door, you'd be as likely to find yourself in a cave as you would a person's living room.

The ramshackle picket fence had a sign nailed to it:

Keep Out Unless You Have a Scheduled Appointment

I ignored this, entered the garden anyway, and knocked on the door.

Nothing.

Waggery jiggled the lock with his beak, eager to put his lock-picking skills to work.

"Not now," I said.

I knocked again. When there was still no answer, I remembered the girl in the cloak. Baba was probably giving her a reading and didn't want to be disturbed. After all, I didn't have an appointment. I was breaking the rules.

I took a seat on Baba's front porch; Waggery waddled around her yard. I formulated my apology. It would have to be good, as I didn't want anyone in Mariner's Cove to have a problem with me. I was hoping to have a long, happy life here, even if the plan now was to continue going back and forth to Prosperity.

The serene silence, the dim light, and my lingering hang-over made for a soporific combination.

I awoke much later. Waggery was nestled next to me, snoring softly.

"Oh, no," I said, pulling myself together.

"Oh, no," Waggery said, copying me. He shook his feathers.

I could still see some sky through the tops of the trees, so it wasn't fully dark yet. Looking at the sky gave me no indication of how much of the afternoon I had snoozed away. It was always gray in Mariner's Cove, which gave it a relaxing, out-of-time feel. The effect was significantly creepier to wake up in a witch's yard and not know how long I'd been out.

And what of the redhead in the gray cloak? Had she stepped over me on her way out?

I was concerned about my safety. Since I wasn't sure what time it was, I didn't know how much light was left in the day—and I didn't want to risk stumbling down the hill in the dark. I stood up and pounded on Baba's door.

"Baba, it's me, Carrie, from the pirate party at Think Ink last night," I shouted. "I'm so sorry to disturb you like this, without an appointment. I wanted to apologize and explain what I'm doing here. I'm hoping we can sort this out."

Silence.

Waggery made a ding-dong sound, like a doorbell.

"Baba?"

Nothing.

"I guess we're going in," I said. I turned the doorknob and it opened.

I stepped into Baba's parlor.

My jaw dropped.

Where Aunt Inez's house—now mine—was crisp corners, neutral colors, and tidy, dust-free surfaces, Baba's was a profusion of fabrics, posters, crystal balls, velvet furnishings, and a collection of antique fortune telling games and framed photos that appeared to be authentic spiritualist images from the Victorian era. She had rune stones carved from obsidian and a glass case filled with an impressive variety of tarot cards. I spied at least ten Ouija boards. One wall was decorated with framed covers of *Tea Leaves* magazine featuring Baba in various turbans, caftans, and scarves.

Wait. Baba was famous?

Why didn't Stormy warn me? I arrived in Mariner's Cove thinking I'd be the first of my kind.

Waggery inspected himself in one of her twenty or more gold-framed mirrors and pecked at his reflection.

"Not now, Wags," I said. "This isn't ours, and I can't afford to replace it if you break it. Not to mention we don't need seven years' bad luck. What the—" I leaned in closer to the mirror.

A foot? Was it attached to a leg?

I turned around to find a heap of fabric on the floor. A heap of fabric with a foot sticking out.

I moved in for a closer look. This was no pile of fabric. This was Baba Caracatiţă. And it didn't require psychic powers to see she was dead.

Chapter Five

The police, EMTs, and at least one volunteer firefighter whom I met the night before (and who went by the pirate-name, Golly Roger) crammed shoulder-to-shoulder into Baba's parlor. Calling them had been tricky. I explained repeatedly to the dispatcher how they'd need to ascend the hill on a narrow trail I'd only recently learned about myself. After hanging up, Waggery and I waited on the front porch because I saw no benefit to staying in a room with a dead body.

I peered through the window as the police swept the surfaces for evidence. The place was tiny and overstuffed, and they were making a mess of everything and stumbling all over each other.

Keeping Waggery calm while all of Baba's shiny objects and interesting relics were being overturned was a challenge. He flapped and squirmed, eager to get inside to join in the fuss.

A tall, heavyset man with a bristle-brush mustache appeared in front of me. "I'm Officer Maigret," he said. "We can't seem to find the kitchen."

"What?"

"Ms.—" he looked at his notes "Karah-sah-teeta? Her kitchen. Where is it?" He squinted at me.

"This is the first time I've been here," I said. "I came up the same path you did. I let myself in, looked around for about sixty seconds, saw her foot sticking out of the closet, and immediately called you. And my girlfriend, Stormy Portwood."

"What were you and your, uh, crow doing here, Ms. Dettwiler?"

For the second time in the span of a year, I found myself at the receiving end of an officer's questions about my involvement in a suspicious death.

I didn't like it any better this time around. Stormy and I had already been through the ringer trying to solve two murders in Prosperity. The lies, gossip, suspicion, and in-fighting nearly broke us, not to mention the grief at having lost two of my best friends, one of whom was Stormy's estranged father, Mayor Preston Brix. Stormy and my new relationship were the only good that came out of the last terrible situation. I was already desperate to steer clear of this Baba business if for no other reason than I wanted us to be able to focus on deepening our relationship.

"He's a raven," I said, hoping Waggery's cuteness would soften the officer's attitude toward me. As if on cue, Waggery fluffed his feathers and meowed.

"I came to apologize," I continued.

"Apologize?" the officer asked.

"Yes, sir. Last night, at a pirate party at my girlfriend's tattoo studio—Think Ink downtown—Baba told me to leave Mariner's Cove. I'd had too much rum and mead, and I responded by saying I would make her walk the plank."

"You did what?"

"It made a lot more sense in the context of the party. There were pirates there."

"Like the one behind you?"

"Hey, hey! What's happening here?" It was Titanic Jones. Stormy stood behind him, his shadow eclipsing her. "Officer Maigret, what do you need with Carrie?"

"I'm questioning this witness, Titanic," Maigret said. "Strictly procedure. She found the body."

"You okay?" Stormy asked.

I nodded.

"She came to apologize, Officer Maigret," Stormy said. "I can vouch for her. Titanic told her last night she should come to parley."

"Right," Maigret said. "Parley. Of course. You were playing pirate and pirate time led to a death threat. To a woman who is now dead. Sounds like a perfectly normal night in Mariner's Cove."

"She threatened me first," I said.

Maigret scribbled in his notepad.

"I can represent you, Carrie," Titanic said. He handed me a business card, a different one from last night:

Titanic Jones, Attorney at Law.

I looked at him, puzzled. He winked.

Stormy shrugged.

What was this place?

"Let's allow the evidence to speak for Baba," Diving Bill said, suddenly appearing in the doorway. He wore a navy-blue sweater with an ivory anchor on it. It looked so warm and cozy, I had to stop myself from petting him and asking him to hand it over because I was cold. Again.

He continued. "I'll release my findings after I conduct an autopsy. It would be irresponsible to speculate about her cause of death until then."

Since he was the coroner and dealt with death as his job, it would be easy to assign Diving Bill the attributes of the Death card. Like the Death card, he rides in, dressed in official garb and flying a flag of authority, to deliver a message of endings and transformation. It's the most misunderstood card in the deck. Only a few months prior, the Death card had hoodwinked me into believing my client, Miriam Cringe, was responsible for a grisly murder, and I'm a professional who knows better. Fortunately, the truth came out.

Though I'd only met him twice, I had a feeling Diving Bill, with his authority and confidence, was an ideal expression of the King of Swords. He sat on a throne of competence, and he used his sword to cut through confusion and emotional upheaval. Like a coroner would, quite literally, use a scalpel to find the truth about a person's cause of death.

"There was a woman," I spat out as soon as I remembered. "There was a woman in a gray cloak on the path ahead of me. I saw her briefly before she disappeared into the woods."

"A woman in a cloak?" Stormy asked. "What did she look like?"

"Long red hair, gray cloak," I said. "Like I said, she evaporated. I assumed she was inside getting a reading, and that's why Baba didn't answer when I knocked. I sat down on the front porch with Waggery to wait, and we both fell asleep."

"You fell asleep?" Officer Maigret asked. "You didn't see this woman enter or leave?"

"No, sir," I said.

"Interesting you would see a mysterious stranger on your way to the home of a woman you threatened with murder," said Officer Maigret. "How convenient you fell asleep when she would have been leaving. Did you think of this story on your way here?"

"You don't have to answer, Carrie," Titanic said. "Officer Maigret, is Carrie under arrest?"

"Listen, Maigret," Diving Bill said. "Let's put a pin in this for now. Let me do my work before you go worrying the townsfolk."

Officer Maigret closed his notepad. "Okay, Bill," he said. "We're going to continue our investigation. And Ms. Dettwiller? Stay close. It would be very suspicious if you left town."

"She knows the drill," Stormy said. "It's not her first rodeo."

"Stormy!" I was shocked she'd reference her father's death in this context. "How could you say such a thing?"

"Don't worry, Carrie," Diving Bill said. "The evidence seems clear."

"Does it?"

"Yes. I think you can relax," he said. "I'm sure you had nothing to do with this. But let me know if you find out anything about the woman in a cloak."

Chapter Six

My head felt like it was inside a ringing bell. Eyepatches and grog, dead fortune tellers, wind-chill that cut to bone, tattoos and tarot cards, mysterious fog-colored, red-headed apparitions—everything swirled through my mind in a kaleidoscope of confusion.

"Why do *I* need to find out about the woman in the cloak? It's not my job to solve potential crimes in Mariner's Cove. I don't even have a real job in Mariner's Cove. Unlike the rest of you, who seem to have multiple professions."

We sat in Stormy's flat, warming our bones in front of her hand-stacked river stone fireplace. Titanic made tea in the kitchen. Waggery made a mess of his fruit cup, flinging seeds here and there. The only good news we'd had all day was that Waggery was finally able to keep his food down.

I felt agitated and unnerved, alternatively pacing and sitting, wringing my hands, and gnawing at my nails. All I wanted was to sink into Stormy's sumptuous sofa and let the sound of the churning sea lull me to sleep.

She'd wildly exaggerated when describing her home as 'win-dowless.' While there weren't windows with planter boxes on every wall like at my cottage, the entire sea-facing wall of Stormy's loft was a frosted glass garage door that lifted overhead to reveal a broad balcony with whitewater views and a gas firepit. Initially, I'd hoped this would be where we spent our evenings, bundled up from the chill, sipping Hoggarty Heaven wine and watching the sun sink into the horizon.

But not today, unfortunately.

"Isn't finding mysterious women the purview of Mariner's Cove's finest?" I asked.

"They're volunteers for the most part, too," Titanic called in from the kitchen. "Officer Maigret is also the art therapist at the senior center."

"Anyway, what I want to know, even though I'm definitely staying out of this, is more about Baba," I said. "Did either of you know anything about her before?"

The teacup Titanic gave me was tiny in his hand. He sat down and joined us by the hearth.

"I may've seen her around a couple of times," he said. "I'm not sure, though, and if I did, I never gave her much thought. There are several leftover hippies in Mariner's Cove who look like her—turbans, caftans, her whole witchy, earth-mother vibe. Whether it was her I saw, or any number of other mature ladies who dress in a similar way, is impossible to know now. Plus, I'm a man who enjoys exceedingly good luck, so I've never needed to have my fortune told."

"What about you, Stormy?" I asked. "You must've known. You drew me a map."

"I was as surprised as you were when she barged in last night," she said. "Like Titanic said, she must have blended in. I had no clue we had a full-time fortune teller here in Mariner's Cove. As far as the map goes, I only knew about the deer trail. I thought you'd get frustrated and come home."

"You gave me a faulty map purpose?" My stomach churned. "Why?"

"I didn't expect you to go into the actual forest," she said, more defensively than I liked. "I thought you'd get to the edge, get spooked, and come home. Then we'd figure it out together, later."

This was not the explanation I was hoping for. After the turn of events a few months ago, when we mistakenly attributed guilt to one another, Stormy and I agreed we weren't going to behave suspiciously anymore. I was angry with her, but I didn't want to argue in front of Titanic.

"So, neither of you, long-time residents of Mariner's Cove, had any connection with Baba Caracatiță until last night?" I asked. "Weird." And unbelievable, I wanted to add.

"Maybe she wanted to fly under the radar," Titanic said. "I get it. We do the same with The Shipwrecks. We don't want people to know."

"This feels different," I said. "Fortune telling is how she made her money. Why wouldn't she be more prominent in town? I'm forever joining clubs and going to marketing seminars to drum up tarot business in Prosperity. It's a lot of work. Fortune telling and tarot card reading are niche industries."

"You have a point," Stormy said. "Just because Titanic and I aren't in the know doesn't mean the rest of Mariner's Cove didn't know about her. I mean, there are people in Prosperity who don't know you."

"True," I said. "I had nothing to do with Baba or anything else, so I'm going to stay out of it. Onward."

"It's sad," Stormy said. "I didn't know her, but that doesn't mean I don't feel sorry she's gone. I dug her whole mami-swami thing."

We sat in silence, sipping our tea and thinking about a woman we would never know.

"I know you don't want to get involved," Stormy said after a few minutes. "The woman in the gray cloak seems important, don't you think?"

"No," I said. "I'm going to get through the next few days, keep my head down, and wait for the drama to pass."

"Maybe she's a ghost," Titanic said, deadly serious. "Mariner's Cove is filled with the sad souls of those who perished on the rocks and in the churning waters."

His eyes welled up with tears.

It would be impossible to not love Titanic Jones. He was a King of Cups card if ever I'd met one. In my deck, The King of Cups perches atop a stone throne in the midst of a roiling sea. The ocean seethes around him; a fish leaps out of a wave. In the distance, a sailing ship heralds news and luck. He is the embodiment of calm in the storm, a man who expresses his emotions, but is never controlled by them.

"Describe the ghost lady again," Stormy asked. "Maybe it's someone we know."

"Until we determine she's a ghost, it's better for my sanity if we can agree she's a flesh-and-blood woman," I said. "You should go find her yourself. I want no part of it."

"You're no fun," Stormy said.

"The cloak was basically the same color as the weather here," I said. "It was hard to get a good look. Everything was murky, and she was up the hill in front of me. I think she was of average height. Her skin seemed pale, but 'pale' describes everyone in Mariner's Cove."

"Hey!" said Titanic. "I've been described as 'swarthy.'"

"True, but you are an honest-to-god pirate, professional shipwreck security professional, and attorney at law, so you break all the molds," I said.

"Was the hood up or down?" Stormy asked.

"How did you know there was a hood?"

"No reason," she said, getting up to refill her mug. "Someone says 'cloak' and I think 'what's the point of a cloak without a hood?' It's all very druid."

"Oh," I said. "She did have a hood, though. And you're right. I did say 'cloak,' not 'cape.'"

"You didn't see her hair, then?" she asked.

"I mentioned earlier she was a redhead."

"Would you look at the time?" Titanic said, standing up. "Turns out I've got somewhere to be. Carrie, you let me know if you want to talk things through."

"Thanks, Titanic," I said. "Like I said, I don't want any part of this. I'll be hiding out here until they finish the investigation."

"I won't charge you for advice," he said. "If you're wondering."

"No, not at all," I said, a half-truth. I didn't have the funds to pay for an attorney before I was even suspected of anything. "I don't want to look like I'm butting in where I don't belong. The pros can take it from here."

"Suit yourself," he said. "Stormy, I'm still glad you called. If you change your mind, you can find me at The Shipwrecks."

"Or in your very traditional and formal office in the center of Main Street, Monday through Friday from nine a.m. until five p.m." Stormy said. "Weirdo."

"Arrgh," Titanic said. He winked as Stormy closed the door on him.

"He's an interesting guy," I said. "One of the most interesting people I've met, other than you, in a very long time."

She sat next to me and took my hand in hers.

"You've been through so much," she said. "Let's spend the evening here, you and me. And Waggery. We'll hang out. I'll make some dinner. For us, I mean. Looks like Waggery's done with his."

"I'm starving," I said, realizing I hadn't eaten anything since I woke up. "Can you make grilled cheese?"

"Of course," she said. "Then, after you're fueled up, we should discuss how you're going to spend the next few days here."

"I guess I can't leave until Diving Bill makes his final assessment, huh?"

"In that case, let's hope he takes forever," she said, kissing my hand.

"I'm going to treat it like a holiday." I stretched out on the sofa. "I'm under no suspicion. I have no dog in this fight, as they say, so maybe we can spend a few days cuddled up here. Or you can take me out to The Shipwrecks. I've got to take pictures for Grist. He's going to lose his mind."

"Hey," she said. "Where's your ring?"

My ring. It wasn't on my finger.

"Oh, no!" Waggery said.

We turned over sofa cushions, opened drawers, and upended my suitcase.

Had I been wearing it when I left in the morning?

We searched the flat. Flipped over my luggage. Crawled under the bed.

My ring was gone.

"I guess I know what I'll be doing first thing tomorrow," I said as Stormy rifled through the drawers in the kitchen.

"What?" she asked.

"Retracing my steps to Baba's. I've got to find out if I dropped it, if I absentmindedly put it somewhere, or if it was stolen." I knew finding my ring was a fool's errand, but I couldn't sit here doing nothing when there was the tiniest chance of locating it.

"How could it have been stolen?" she asked.

"The woman in the cloak. I was sleeping, remember?'

"Oh, wow," she said. "Let's hope you dropped it, and we can find it tomorrow."

"Let's hope so," I said. "Because I'd rather spend my day hunting for a ring than hunting for a ghost."

§

"We live in a vast, bountiful, and loving universe," Aunt Inez told me. "Tarot is one way for our souls to communicate with us. It's quite simple. Yet not simple at all."

"Always with these paradoxes and metaphors," I said. "It's confusing and I don't think it's worth it."

I'd reached the point in my tarot training where it was time to level up or remain an amateur. Aunt Inez had presented me a new schedule with more rigorous study, trickier exercises, and more journaling, more reading, more...everything. I was a teenager. Not only did I want to sit around and watch TV all day, but the kids at school called me a witch on the daily, and I wasn't interested in confirming their suspicions.

I didn't want to do what she expected of me. I wanted to argue.

"You're not going to like what I'm about to say," she said. She lowered her purple star-shaped glasses and locked her eyes on mine. "I'm going to say it anyway because you are apparently at the age where I have to start sharing uncomfortable truths for your own good."

I squirmed. Her words felt like a veiled threat. I knew every-thing. What could she possibly tell me for my own good?

"You're wrong," she said. "You're dead wrong."

"What do you mean, I'm wrong?" The fight welled up in me. Aunt Inez and I had always had an overly pleasant relationship,

more like two old friends than a parent and child. I'd never felt anything close to anger with her before.

"You know a little tarot and you've decided it's not worth your time? Wrong."

"It's all random," I said with a whine in my voice. I was repeating what Daisy, a girl at school, had said about my tarot readings. "It's not real."

Aunt Inez sat back. "What's not real?"

"Tarot is all made up. That's what the kids at school say. They think it's stupid."

"Carrie," she began, her tone much softened. "It's not made up. It's not magic. And it's not psychic, not like you think. It's also not random. The cards reveal themselves exactly as they should. It's your job to interpret the story. I'm willing to teach you those skills. You need to meet me halfway by taking your studies seriously."

"How is it not random, though?"

"Carrie, how many times have you gotten the exact same card in a reading for the exact same question?"

It happened all the time. I shrugged like I didn't care.

"It's common," she said. "Do you know why?"

I shrugged again, even though I was interested.

"I mentioned before that the universe is intelligent and abundant."

"Yes?"

"The cards are one way it communicates with us."

I sighed.

Aunt Inez got up from the table. "I sense you aren't in a place where you're ready to hear the truth."

"What's the truth?" I asked.

"The cards reassure us that every second we're alive is an opportunity to learn, heal, receive, and grow. There's nothing *random about it. You'll understand when you get further in your studies."*

"How do you know?"

"Because your cards told me."

§

Chapter Seven

"Wake up, Buttercup," I whispered to Stormy as I gently shook her. "It's still early. Good time to go ring hunting."

Stormy's not a morning person. To her credit, she got right up, got dressed, and was ready to go.

"Impressive," I said. "I think it's a record. You want coffee before we go?"

"No," she said. "I couldn't sleep. I was so worried about your ring. Let's hurry."

I loved this aspect of Stormy—her willingness to jump in and get the job done.

"Right behind you," I said. "Going to give Wags a quick bite and then we can go. I was up all night, too."

Stormy stopped in her tracks and held a finger up.

I leaned toward her. "I don't hear anything."

"Spike," she grumbled. "I'll be in the shop."

She ran out of the flat, and I heard her boots on the stairs.

I put on my denim jacket. "Time to go," I said, and Waggery hopped onto my shoulder. "Let's go see what a Spike is."

At the bottom of the stairs, a freckled boy wearing a

Mariner's Cove Smugglers little league uniform stood in the doorway of Think Ink. His chin jutted out, and his hands were on his hips.

"Get out. Now."

"Gimme a tattoo."

"You're too young," she said.

"My mom said it was okay."

"Not true. And even if your mother asked me to tattoo your whole backside, I couldn't do it. It's illegal to tattoo children, Spike. Plus, we're leaving."

"We are in a hurry," I said, trying to help.

He eyed me. "Who the hell are you?"

Waggery growled.

"Manners, Spike," Stormy said. "This is Carrie. Now go away and don't come back until you're eighteen."

Stormy made a move to corral him through the door, but he ducked around her.

"Is he real?" he asked, pointing at the raven.

"Yes. This is Waggery," I said. "He bites."

Waggery stared him down. Spike pretended to lose interest and wandered toward my table. I sat down, pulled my cards from my pocket, and shuffled.

"Solitaire?" he asked.

I got an idea.

"I'm a tarot card reader. Want to try?"

Stormy tapped her watchless wrist. "We need to go."

I motioned for her to calm down.

"Have a seat, Spike."

I shuffled the cards and asked him to pull one.

"So cool," he said, tracing his finger on the image on the card.

"It's The Sun," I said. "See the baby on the back of a horse, the sun beaming down on him? That's you, Spike."

"It's awesome." He touched the card with a grubby finger. "The baby's naked! Funny."

"It is funny," I agreed. "It's also a 'yes' card."

I saw Stormy out of the corner of my eye. "Carrie," she said, her voice a warning. "What game are you playing?"

"It's no game, Stormy." I turned my attention back to Spike. "Tarot cards provide guidance. And this one? To me, it says Stormy's being a big, boring dud and should give you—the cute, adorable sun baby—the tattoo he wants."

"Carrie, I swear," Stormy muttered through gritted teeth.

"Couldn't have put it better myself," Spike said.

"Can I see another one?" he asked.

"In tarot, that's called a 'clarification.' You pull a new card to get more information about your question."

"I didn't ask a question," he said. "You told me to pull a card."

"Touché," Stormy mumbled, loud enough for me to hear it.

"Pull a card, Spike."

He did so.

"Cool," he said.

"The Page of Wands," I said. Since this wasn't a real reading (an ethical breach, but a minor one), I took a few liberties with the meaning. I had an agenda. "A good luck card, usually. In your case, Spike, it shows you holding this staff. And the staff is magic. It gives you one wish."

"Carrie, so help me—"

"I see it," Spike whispered. "Amazing."

"Are you ready to make your wish, Spike?"

He was awe-struck. "Yes," he whispered.

"Go ahead." I folded my hands and waited silently.

"I wish." He cleared his throat. "I wish my stepdad would go back to his other family."

I'd miscalculated. Stormy slammed cabinet doors and

stomped and sighed. How was I going to finesse this? What had begun as a way to get Spike out of our way was morphing into something else.

"Spike, let's try a wish that only pertains to you. This is your one shot, and we need to hurry. Are you sure you want to waste it on yucky old—"

"Todd."

"Exactly. Why waste a perfectly good wish on Todd? Ask for what you really want, Spike."

"What I really want?"

"Why did you come in here?"

"Oh! I wish Stormy would give me a tattoo!"

"Precisely!" I shouted. "Stormy, do you have your special pen ready? Spike's leaving here with a tattoo today. And then he's not coming back."

Stormy lifted her head. "The special pen—. Right!"

I loved it when Stormy caught on.

"Really?" Spike said.

"Come on over," she said.

"Stormy, you're going to have to warn his mom first," I said through closed teeth.

"Do I look like I'd vandalize a child without parental permission?"

I raised a brow.

"You have a point," she said. "Hey, Spike, what's your mom's number?"

Spike produced his phone and held it to his ear. "Mom? I'm getting a tattoo!"

"Easy there," Stormy said, taking the phone. "Spike's mom? Sorry to call so early."

She sauntered to the other side of the room to connive with Spike's mother in secret. When she returned, she was brandishing a permanent marker and looking like she'd had a good laugh.

"We're all set," she said. "Your mom says one and one only. No more until you're eighteen."

"Why would I need another one?" he asked.

"Right," she said, stealing a quick glance at her tattooed arm sleeve in the mirror. "You want a raven?"

"Sure!" he said.

She put his wrist under her magnifying light, and within a few seconds, Spike had his first 'tattoo'—a small raven, its wings outstretched.

"Nice," he said.

Spike turned his wrist back and forth, inspecting the artwork from every angle.

"You should blow on it," Stormy said. "Standard tattoo practice."

"Got it. Thank you!" He ran out of the building and the door closed behind him.

"Another satisfied customer," I said.

"You're here fewer than twenty-four hours and you've already got me inking children," Stormy said.

"What can I say? I'm a rebel."

"Quok," Waggery agreed.

"Ready for another adventure?" I asked.

Stormy pulled me close and gave me a kiss. "Every day is an adventure with you, whether we're tattooing children, searching for lost jewelry, or stumbling over dead bodies."

It wasn't funny, but I laughed anyway.

Chapter Eight

Within a few minutes of Spike's departure, Stormy, Waggery, and I were making our way to Baba's.

"I used to think secret compartments were cool," Stormy said on the path to Baba's, "but secret forest paths are even better."

"You didn't know about her house or the path before yesterday?" I asked again. Something didn't feel right.

"Like I explained, I'd seen the path," she said. "It never occurred to me to follow it into the thicket. I'm sorry I misled you. Believe it or not, I wanted to keep you safe."

I felt my anger rising again. "I know you care, but you can't keep doing things that make you seem untrustworthy. Remember our deal? I need to be able to rely on what you say and what you do. For the record, I'm still upset. And you never thanked me for getting Spike off your back."

"That was ingenious," she said. "Can't believe I never thought of it. So, thank you, Carrie. I appreciate your cleverness. And I promise from now on, I'll only be a straight shooter."

"You're welcome," I said. "You're forgiven."

She did a little dance. "I'm excited to do this hike again. I was in such a hurry to yesterday I didn't have a chance to enjoy myself."

She took off.

"Wait!" I called after her. "We need to take our time so we can spot the ring if I dropped it."

I was discouraged already. Stormy's high spirits would be hard to quell, and that, combined with the fact that the grasses lining the path were ultra-green because of the constant supply of Mariner's Cove moisture, led me to believe finding a needle in a haystack would be easier than finding my beloved emerald ring.

"I'll do my best," she said. "I bet Waggery finds it. He's a divining rod for shiny objects." She stood with her hands on her hips and took in the view (from the half-way point on the path). "I wonder how far up we need to go to see the ocean."

Waggery was subdued, still unsure what to make of this strange situation. He wasn't on a leash, but he stayed close, hopping lightly on the path in front of me, and looking over his shoulder every few feet to make sure I was coming along. Stormy had a point. Waggery had the best chance of finding my ring if I'd lost it here.

"Whoa," Stormy said as we got to the edge of the forest. "When I go adventuring, I normally go to the coast for the cliffs, the tide pools, and The Shipwrecks. But if I'd known Mariner's Cove had inland secrets, I would have headed for the hills more often."

"Keep looking," I said, letting her hear my fretting tone. "It's important we find my ring."

"It's important to me, too," she said. "We'll find it."

We walked silently, save for an occasional *quok* from Waggery or a sigh from Stormy when she saw something pretty. Eventually, we found ourselves standing at Baba's gate.

Stormy jumped right over and began to search the front yard.

She noticed my hesitation and called to me in a stage whisper that did nothing to lower her volume. "Why aren't you coming in? What's wrong?"

"It's a crime scene, Stormy. A woman died here. I understand it's a big, grand adventure. But we shouldn't forget—"

"You're right, Carrie. I'm sorry if I seem insensitive. But we don't know there was any foul play. It's possible she simply croaked."

"I don't know," I said. "It seems so melodramatic. Burst into a pirate party, make demands, give up the ghost at home, with no one around." I shivered. "I think we should find the ring quickly if we can and get out of here. Try not to touch anything."

"Are your psychic powers flaring?" she asked. I could always count on Stormy to be a smart aleck.

"Ugh, not now. If I need to tell one more person I'm not psychic—wait, did you see that?"

"See what?"

"There. In the window."

Stormy took a step toward the house. She squinted. "I don't see anything."

I jumped the gate and ducked down behind the base of a redwood tree. Waggery scurried behind me. "Get down," I whispered. "She might see you."

Stormy squatted behind the wishing well, about five feet away. "Who might see me?" The stage whisper was back.

"She's in the house," I mouthed. "The lady in the gray cloak."

Chapter Nine

I'd never had an experience where my eyes deceived me. I'd never seen a ghost or apparition of any kind, nor did I hear voices. Occasionally, I'd had a dream that seemed prescient, but was likely a coincidence. When I say I saw the gray lady in Baba's house, I meant it, and I was certain. It frightened me. Everyone knows that humans are much more deadly than ghosts. But Stormy? She was an adrenaline junkie, unlikely to back down from spirit, monster, or human.

"We have to go in now," she said, as she sneaked to the front porch. "Is Waggery still picking locks?"

Upon hearing his name and 'picking locks,' Waggery flew to Stormy's side and pecked at the doorknob. Every rattle and clink of the loosening doorknob was a blow dart filled with anxiety hitting me in the chest.

"I don't think it's safe," I said from my hiding spot behind the tree. "I'm staying out of it, remember?"

"We're going in." Stormy turned the doorknob. "It's not even locked!"

"Someone's already in there!"

She and Waggery disappeared inside.

I stood, frozen. If I hadn't been so unutterably terrified, I might have realized I was angry. We had agreed to stay out of trouble. Breaking into a dead woman's house with my pet raven wasn't exactly staying out of trouble.

Stormy poked her head out. "Come on in. There's no one here. I looked under the table and everything. Besides, ghosts aren't real."

Did I detect a smirk on her face?

Waggery perched on her forearm, as if he was trying to convey everything was fine. The sight of the two of them together, eyes shining with mischief, filled me with both love and jealousy. They were adorable, but I didn't want them to be adorable together without me. I shook off my anxiety and joined them in the parlor.

"I'm sure I saw someone in here. I need you to believe me."

"Carrie," she said, taking my hand. "I believe you. But look. This place is so small. There is no way your gray-cloaked specter is hiding in here."

She held up the tablecloth. Then she pulled apart the curtains that covered the closet area where Baba had been lying yesterday.

"See? No room."

"Where's the kitchen?" I asked. "The bedroom? Did Baba spend her whole life in this one tiny room?"

"Unlikely," Stormy said. "A person can barely turn around in here."

"Don't disturb anything," I said. "Let's look for the ring and get out. I guess you didn't see it on the front porch?"

"I did not," she said. "I'm sure Waggery would have grabbed it if it was there."

She walked slowly around the room.

"I didn't get a chance to look at any of this yesterday," she said. "It's astonishing."

I gazed at Baba's collection of framed covers of *Tea Leaves* magazine.

"It's weird," I said. "Her face is familiar."

"Have you seen that magazine before?"

"Of course," I said. "Aunt Inez had a subscription. She liked the crossword puzzle."

"She's been on the cover every couple of years. Probably that's why she looks familiar."

"True," I said.

"These cards." Stormy turned a deck over and over in her hands. "I didn't know there were so many different types of tarot cards. I thought the deck you use is the one everyone uses."

"Not at all," I said. "The Rider Waite deck is the classic deck. But there are decks with faeries, angels, crystals, cats... There are decks of oracle cards and fortune-telling cards for everyone."

Stormy picked up a different deck from Baba's table. "These are incredible."

"You shouldn't be touching anything," I said.

I took a closer look.

"This is a famous deck. It's called *Regina Tentaculelor*." I flipped through the cards.

I was enchanted by the artwork. Images from the Black Sea Coast. Fishermen, sea life, boats, and mariners leaped off each card in vibrant, hand painted hues. The cards were thick and sturdy, but I could feel their age. They lacked the waxy plastic coating of newer decks; they bent a little too willingly. But I couldn't take my eyes off them.

"This is a rare deck," I said. "I'm sure there are copies out there, but I believe this one is the real deal. It feels old. And wise."

"These images are interesting," Stormy said. "I would love

to have some of these as options for Think Ink. Do you think we could—"

"Steal it?" I interrupted. "Not a chance. We shouldn't be touching it."

"How about I snap a few shots with my phone?"

"No way! We're not supposed to be here, remember? Although I would love to do a reading with these."

"Do it." Stormy's eyes were wide and black. It would be hard to talk her out of it. I'd seen this look before.

"I couldn't! They don't belong to me."

"You don't need to do a full, sit-down reading like you do for your customers," she said. "You could pull one card?"

"I could, couldn't I?"

"Do it," she stage-whispered. "Please? One little card? As a treat?"

I could never resist Stormy's thirst for adventure.

"I'm not going to do my full Vegas shuffle," I said, taking a seat in Baba's chair. "I don't want to damage them."

Although I wouldn't have admitted it in that moment, I was practically vibrating with excitement. This was our element, Stormy's and mine. Searching for lost things, sneaking around, solving puzzles, sorting through clues, facing problems head-on and getting things done. I secretly loved every minute of it, but in order to keep her calm, I needed to pretend to be the rational one. Like I was with Spike. You let people get what they want in a way that keeps the guardrails in place, so they remain safe.

But holding those cards? Feeling their weight in my hands after a morning of sleuthing? Total nirvana.

I lightly rearranged the cards to wake them up. "What's our question?"

"Who killed Baba?"

"Stormy," I said. "That's not how this works, and you know

it. How about, 'what should we be aware of as we investigate the truth about Baba?'"

Stormy nodded. "I see now why you're the tarot pro, and I inject people with ink."

I concentrated on the question while I cut the deck into three piles. I pulled the top card and placed it in front of me on the table.

"Here goes nothing," I said and flipped the card.

The Devil. Or as it was written on the card, *Diavolul*.

It was reversed.

"Can't be good," Stormy said.

"It's not what you think. It's not a prediction; it's a warning."

"Explain, please."

"This doesn't mean we're going to hell," I said. "It's letting us know we may have an unhealthy obsession. See these two people chained together?"

"Yikes," she said.

"I'm not saying it's a good luck card because it's not. But rather than letting it spook us, we should listen to its message. When the Devil is upright, it can be seen as an encouragement to have a little fun, to let go of preconceived notions of how you should be. But since it's reversed—"

"It means we're doomed," she said.

"Doomed," Waggery repeated. "Doomed. Doomed."

"See?"

"Ignore the bird," I said. Waggery blew a raspberry and waddled off. "The card is telling us not to get too wrapped up in dangerous pursuits."

"What is a dangerous pursuit?" she asked. "How does one get too wrapped up in it?"

I fought the urge to respond sarcastically about our situation. Was she serious? We were in the house of a dead woman, using her beloved things, while there was an active investigation happening. All of this was a dangerous pursuit. Instead, I said, "Let's not allow ourselves to get carried away."

"Carried away? Are you serious?" Stormy laughed. "I can't believe you said that."

I heard it and had to laugh. "The way you stormied in here shows that you're probably raven mad," I said.

She smacked her forehead. "Can't compete with that," she said. "You broke your own rule about raven puns."

"It's crow references," I said. "Waggery is a raven; I get offended when people make crow jokes. Raven puns are totally on the table."

"Good to know. Carrion."

It felt good to laugh, despite the macabre circumstances. Waggery giggled, too. He hated to be left out.

"Back to business," I said. "I have a hard time understanding readings I do for myself. I bring my own biases. Moving forward, we should be aware we could be in over our heads."

"Got it," she said. "Message received."

"What's weird is this is the second time in two days this card has appeared in my readings."

"What does that mean?"

"I need to pay attention. And not let events get out of control. I don't know exactly what or why yet."

I put the cards back and tapped the Devil card neatly into the middle. I loved seeing this deck, but I wished I hadn't touched it. It wasn't mine. And I didn't love the reading.

"I have to wonder why Baba would use such a rare, delicate deck for her readings," I said. "My cards take a beating. This deck has got to be over a century old and there's no way you wouldn't damage it if you used it every day."

Stormy, who was rarely disturbed by any card reading, had picked up the deck and was flipping through it.

"Yeah. Baba. Old deck. Weird," she said. "Hello. What's

this? Oh my god. Carrie, you have to promise you won't freak out."

"Telling me not to freak out means there is a one-hundred-percent chance I'll freak out," I said. "What did you find?"

"It was stuck to another card," she said. "The Chariot."

She handed me a business card. It read:

RAVENOUS PARTNERS
Building Prosperity One Donation at a Time
(707) 843-2222

The breath left my body. "I'm officially freaked out," I said. Ravenous Partners was the sort-of-secret group my Aunt Inez and Uncle Grist had been working with to re-imagine the town of Prosperity. The group had a falling out, then two members were murdered. I didn't like the name showing up in these circumstances, and I hoped it was a strange, but explainable, coincidence.

"Flip it over," she said, not breaking eye contact with me.

"You're scaring me now."

I looked at the back of the card.

This rare deck should be in your collection. Thanks for everything, E.I.

If I'd been standing, seeing this handwriting would have knocked me off my feet.

"Inez," I whispered. The words were a punch in the gut.

"No," Stormy said, walking around to my side of the table. "It says E.I. Obviously, someone from Ravenous Partners gifted Baba this octopus deck. Do you know anyone whose name starts with E?"

"It's Aunt Inez. I'd recognize her handwriting anywhere," I

said. "Her nickname among her friends was Evil I. E.I. It was an inside joke she shared with her friends."

"Whoa."

"I know." I turned the card over a few more times in my hand and then pocketed it.

"Any significance that this Ravenous Partners business card came attached to the chariot card?"

"Oh, um, there could be more to it," I began. "In tarot, we pay attention to what's called 'jumpers.' These are cards that fall out of a deck while you're shuffling or moving the cards. You can ignore them, of course. But some in the practice believe jumpers have additional significance."

"This chariot didn't jump out, though, did it?" Stormy looked disappointed.

"Not exactly. But if we were to decide the card was meaningful, the chariot suggests we're on the right track."

"I'll take it," she said. "I'm wondering, though—"

"Yes?"

"What's the business card about? Is this the kind of thing a coroner would need to know? Should we get Diving Bill on the phone? Show him this?"

I could tell by the twinkle in her eye she was goading me. I'd been steadfast in my decision to stay out of this mess. Resolute. Immovable.

But now?

I was torn. But I was keeping this business card.

I didn't let Stormy see me waver, though.

"I'm not sure if this would affect his investigation," I said. "I don't think it's a good idea to let anyone know we were breaking and entering the day after Baba's body was found under suspicious circumstances. Nor should we mention the clue that possibly ties us and members of our families to the deceased."

"You're getting involved," she sang. Waggery bounced up

and down in the corner. They were becoming co-conspirators, and despite the enormous stress of Baba's murder and the loss of my ring, I could see how cute they were together.

"I don't like all this stealing," I said. "However, we need to figure out what's going on before implicating ourselves and our families—both living and deceased. They were trying to build a business in Prosperity, so maybe Baba was in talks with them to come there, help with Prosperity's future? Or maybe they were going to help her in some way?"

"A pretty big leap, but it's not impossible," she said. "I don't want to add fuel to the fire, but Baba could've known my dad. He was the mayor of Prosperity, but he did visit me here when it was convenient for him. And he was always schmoozing."

I shivered at the thought. I wanted there to be no connection, nothing to see, and to forget any of this was happening.

"Quok!"

Waggery was making a fuss across the room.

"What is it?" I asked. He was pecking at the floor.

"No touching," I said. "Waggery, it's a crime scene."

I walked over to see what was troubling him.

"Oh wow, Stormy," I said. "Get ready to freak out. Again."

"What is it?" she asked.

"A flash drive."

The flash drive was a glittery purple—the exact kind of thing Waggery would spot anywhere.

"You think this has anything good on it?" Stormy asked.

The desire to snatch the drive out of her hand, run home, and read everything on it was powerful. Instead, I took it from her and put it in my pocket to give to Diving Bill later. I silently congratulated myself on my restraint.

"I'm stealing this," I said to her. "I'm going to give it to the authorities."

"Sure thing, boss," Stormy said, rubbing her hands together.

"I'm excited to see what you tell them when they ask how you got it."

I let my silence be my answer. I didn't have a plan.

I couldn't give this flash drive to Diving Bill.

Stormy was having fun. She continued to search.

"We need to get out of here," I said. The hairs on my arms were all at attention, and I had a queasy feeling in my stomach. "C'mon, Waggery."

"Nevermore," he said.

He flew to a beaded sconce on the back wall, landed, and squawked.

As I went to fetch him, I noticed some oddly placed hinges.

Waggery saw them, too. He was eyeballing them like he was sending me a message.

I knew exactly what I was looking at. I nodded at him, and he released a quiet purr. My heart swelled. I adored Waggery. Until Stormy came along, it was the two of us. Working together like this reminded me that, even if he was getting close to Stormy, we'd still have a deep connection. Unbreakable.

Waggery was so excited, he let out a "Whoopee!"

"What's happening over there?" Stormy asked.

"You like secret compartments and hidden trails?" I asked in a breezy, offhand tone.

"You bet I do," she said.

"Get over here, then," I said, fully giving up on the idea I was going to be able to divorce myself from any part of this Baba drama. "Because Baba's got a fake bookshelf."

Chapter Ten

Stormy had been correct when she told Officer Maigret that this wasn't my first rodeo. I'd been involved in a murder investigation before, and I'd solved it because of my experiences with hidden tunnels, long-held secrets, and hidden compartments. Growing up in Prosperity, my buddy Hank and I had created adventure everywhere we went, from his family's opulent estate to the dusty vineyards that blanketed the areas outside of town. We were cowboys, astronauts, prospectors, and, yes, even pirates. My thirst for adventure was as finely tuned as Stormy's in some ways. But after I became responsible for Aunt Inez's home and Waggery, I had more to lose and approached life more cautiously.

But seeing this secret door? I nearly yelped with joy.

Calmly, of course, and with reverence.

It was exactly as you would imagine—a find straight out of a murder mystery set in an imposing old mansion at the end of a rarely traveled, windswept lane. This bookshelf, filled with leather bound collections of Agatha Christie, Edgar Allan Poe, L. Frank Baum, and Arthur Conan Doyle books, was a door.

"How can you tell?" Stormy leaned in for a closer look.

"Over here." I pointed to a barely concealed row of hinges on the right side of the shelf.

"Oh, I see it now," she said. "Good eye."

"Waggery found them, natch. Give that ornate wall sconce a tug."

Stormy, so giddy she could barely contain herself, danced over to Baba's light fixture and yanked on it. "It's not working," she said.

She pulled it again and frowned.

I smiled at her.

"Oh, you!" she said. "You got me, Dettwiler. I didn't think you had it in you."

"I contain multitudes," I said. "Here's what Waggery was looking at. A lock. Hidden in the binding of this fake book."

"*The Murders in the Rue Morgue*," Stormy read. "A bit on the nose, isn't it?"

"It would appear Baba had a literary sense of humor."

"What do you think is behind there?" she asked. "A slide into a snake pit? A moat full of crocodiles? Glitter bomb?"

"I was thinking a small kitchen? Maybe a rice cooker?"

"You're probably right," she said. "How do we open it?"

"We need a hairpin or a paperclip. Something metal and malleable. Waggery is magic with locks."

We looked around the room.

"This woman's got a hundred decks of cards, sixty-eight crystal balls, at least a thousand scarves, and every kind of fortune telling implement I've heard of and many I haven't, and not one paperclip," Stormy said.

"Guess when you've got the magic arts at your fingertips, you don't need such uninteresting, workaday items."

I heard a jingling sound and turned to see that Waggery had a keychain in his beak.

"The shiny-object fascination comes in handy yet again," I said. "Look who came through for us."

Waggery dropped the key on its raven-shaped keyring in my hand. "Interesting," I said. "It's a raven."

Stormy rubbed her hands together. "I'm dying to get into whatever is behind the secret door."

"Be careful what you wish for," I said and pushed the key into the lock.

The door swung open.

I couldn't believe what I saw.

"What the—" Stormy said, taking a step through the doorway.

A steep, narrow staircase led to a sunny landing. I couldn't see what was at the top of the stairs.

Stormy barreled up.

"This is, like, the third coolest thing I've ever done," she called over her shoulder.

Waggery and I followed and took our time. I was half concerned about what we were going to find, and half wanting to savor this strange, spooky occurrence.

I took my final step.

My gob was officially smacked.

After our talk of snake pits, moats, explosives, and kitchens, nothing could have prepared me for what we actually found.

"It's a—wow," Stormy said.

I let it sink in. "I know," I said, looking around in disbelief.

"It's a regular suburban house." Stormy said. "And this door looks like it leads to a regular boring coat closet."

§

I'd finished a practice reading when Aunt Inez gave me a piece of advice I still grapple with today.

"*Do you know what I mean when I say 'beginner's mind'?*" *She asked me.*

I was fifteen and knew everything. "*Of course.*"

"*Why don't you explain it to me?*"

"*When I started learning tarot, I had beginner's mind. I was new at it. But now, I'm an expert.*"

Her wry smile let me know she was about to say something she wanted me to remember.

"*You're an expert now?*" *I knew she didn't expect an answer.* "*Good. Then this next bit should come as no surprise. Approach every reading with beginner's mind.*"

"*I'm not a beginner.*"

"*Every time I read for a client, I do my best to approach the spread as if I am a beginner.*"

"*You're not a beginner, either. You've probably forgotten more about tarot than most people will ever know.*"

She laughed, which I loved.

"*When we approach a task with beginner's mind—a term taken from Zen Buddhism—it means we leave behind what we think we already know. We drop assumptions. We allow the information to enter our thoughts without adding any preconceived ideas. We behave as though this is the first time we've ever read cards.*"

"*That's dishonest. I know what the cards mean. Usually. Because I'm an expert.*"

"*When we think we know everything, we make mistakes,*" *she said.* "*I'm not suggesting you forget what you know about the cards. I'm suggesting you leave your mind open. You'll get to know your clients over the years. Let each reading be separate. Don't press your opinion on them or try to steer them in any way. Take in the information you have and present it to them as if it's brand new.*"

I was too young to grasp the nuance of what she was telling me. I'd spent several months applying myself to my study of tarot in a disciplined way, memorizing details about colors, symbolism, and numerology, only to have her tell me to pretend to know nothing.

"You look like a deer in headlights," she said. "Everything okay?"

I'd never heard that expression before. I smiled. "Yeah. I'm fine."

"It's like school," she said. "You're learning a whole bunch of stuff you might think is useless. But one day, you're going to face a problem that requires a beginner's mind, no preconceived notions, and you're going to be glad you know how to do it. Trust me. It happens to all of us. When we're able to let go of outcomes and only deal with what's right in front of us—that's how you find treasure."

§

Chapter Eleven

"I've never seen anything so bizarre," Stormy said. "I say this as I realize one of my best friends is a pirate lawyer and my girlfriend is a tarot card reader with a lock-picking raven."

"I'm curious how the design of the house works," I said. "How did we come up that trail, through those witchy woods, through a dilapidated old garden, and into a parlor straight out of a Victorian spiritualist's dream, while this entirely normal house appears to be situated on the least interesting cul-de-sac in a neighborhood where original ideas, style, and interesting architecture go to die?"

She traced her finger along the beige counter tile, turned on and off the perfectly forgettable stainless-steel faucet, opened the mid-range white refrigerator, and eyed its mediocre contents: eggs, milk, butter.

"Who lives here?"

"I'm guessing Baba," I said. "From the look of things, she was living a double life."

"You can say that again," said Stormy. "Look at what's in the driveway."

Waggery and I joined her by the utterly unexceptional bay window that looked out over a regular, well-mown green lawn.

"Whoa," I said, not believing what I saw. "Baba drives a Subaru."

"I didn't see that one coming," Stormy said.

Dazed, I wandered into the bedroom. "If you think the Subaru is unexpected, you should see what's in here."

I'd found Baba's closet.

"So much neutral," Stormy said. "It's a rainbow of neutral shades. Everything from beige to ecru, eggshell, and beyond."

"Don't forget cream and off-cream," I said. "Here's a blinding collection of dove gray, slate, and river stone."

"What's happening here?" Stormy asked. "Did we step into an alternate universe?"

"Baba Caracatiță: Gaudy, melodramatic fortune teller on some days; low-key-lady-who-wants-nothing-more-than-to-blend-in on other days. There's not a single scarf, turban, or caftan to be found in this wardrobe."

"Why?" Stormy asked.

"I couldn't possibly figure that out right now," I said. "This blah wardrobe could explain why so many of you didn't know about Baba. Dressed in these clothes," I pulled out an ivory fleece anorak, "she could have easily moved through Mariner's Cove without anyone so much as looking up from their coffee."

"So, she didn't walk around dressed as Baba all the time."

I could see Stormy putting the puzzle pieces together.

"I'm so confused," I said. "If she was threatened by me and my tiny tarot business at your shop, wouldn't it have behooved her to make a name for herself, to get people up here for readings and whatever else she offered? Her aggressive presence certainly got my attention. I bet I would have come for a reading too. I can see the appeal, even if it's a different service than what Aunt Inez taught me to offer."

"Baba was aggressive?" Stormy arched a brow. "I seem to remember a certain someone getting in her face and threatening her."

"Can we forget all of that?"

"Never," she said. "If you're going to prove she was—or wasn't—murdered, you're going to need to prove you're not a suspect."

"True," I said. "How do I prove I didn't kill someone and possibly find who did, if I don't even know the true identity of the person who was murdered? Or why she has a business card linking her to my aunt's old business in her desk?"

"We need to walk around the house," Stormy said. "Check out how it's configured. There's got to be some kind of switcheroo, like a secret tunnel or hidden cave."

"I'm right behind you," I said. "First, we'd better find Waggery."

We emerged from Baba's bedroom. I was still feeling overwhelmed by the underwhelming decor Baba had chosen for her home.

"I bet Baba isn't even her real name," Stormy said. "It's probably Carol. Or Vicky. The least interesting person I ever met was named Vicky."

Waggery was piling items in a corner next to Baba's fireplace. "What's going on, Waggery?" I asked. "Whatcha got here?"

I sifted through the pile to find the usual suspects. Rubber band. Twist tie. An assortment of coins. And a ring.

I could have cried with joy. "Good boy, Waggery!" I picked him up and gave him a light hug. "You're the best."

He dropped the ring into my hand, wriggled free, and flapped to the kitchen island, where he squatted like he was sitting on a nest. He usually tolerated my hugs, especially when he was being praised, and he nearly always followed up with a kiss. What was the problem?

I looked at the ring.

"Oh, no."

"Oh, no," Waggery said. He sighed and fluffed his feathers.

"Your ring!" Stormy said. "I knew if anyone could find it, Waggery could."

I turned the ring over in my hand.

"It's not mine."

"How do you know? Try it on."

"I can't even squeeze it past my second pinkie knuckle."

"Do rings shrink?"

"It's not mine." I handed it to her.

"Looks identical, though."

I sifted through the pile again for any other clue that might shine a light on what all of this meant. My fingers caught on a very long red hair.

"Look at this," I said, stretching the strand out before me. "I bet it belongs to our ghost."

"Possibly," Stormy said. "I wonder if she had anything to do with Baba's untimely demise."

"Where's my ring?" I asked. My eyes welled with tears. "Waggery found this one within a few minutes. If my ring was in this house, he'd have it by now."

"I don't think we should leave here without it," Stormy said. "I think there's more at play here than a fortune teller passing into the next realm. I'll be more careful. Carrie, I think we're tampering with a crime scene."

"I'm glad you finally see it my way," I said. I caught a glimpse of grey outside the window, a barely perceptible swish of fabric before it disappeared. I waved Stormy to the window.

"Did you see her?" I asked.

"See who?"

"Slight change of plan," I said, opening the front door. Waggery flew to a perch on Baba's standard issue aluminum lamppost, exactly like the ones found in the neighbor's yards.

"We're going ghost-hunting."

Chapter Twelve

"No. This is a terrible idea," Stormy said. She stopped me before I got to the bottom of Baba's front steps. "What if we catch her?"

"That's the point!" I motioned for Waggery to land on my shoulder. "To catch her and find out if she has my ring and to ask if she murdered Baba."

"Oh, okay," Stormy said. "You're going to chase a stranger who is likely out running her daily errands, through this neighborhood neither of us have ever seen. And when you catch her, you're going to accuse her of theft and murder?"

"Maybe I haven't thought this through," I said. "Why was she on Baba's path? Why did I think I saw her in the house?"

"She might live here, Carrie. She may have taken the path because it's the quickest way to town without a car. Maybe what you saw was her reflection in Baba's window."

"What about the hair?"

"You never dropped in on a neighbor? And left a feather or two behind without your knowledge? I seem to remember a certain someone's feathers implicating you in the death of my father."

Waggery hid his head in my hair.

"Okay, you're right," I said. "We don't know if Baba's death is suspicious. We don't know anything yet."

"We don't even know how Baba's house is attached to her parlor," she said. "Let's forget the gray ghost for now and figure out what kind of Escher-esque architectural magic is happening."

"You mean we'll descend the stairs and wind up on the first floor again? We'll follow a straight hallway and end where we started? A real-life Escher drawing?" I got swept away thinking about Baba building a house of illusion.

Stormy brought me back. "Let's hope it's as cool as Escher," she said. "It's probably more like her parlor is a converted basement. And woods behind the house conceal the neighborhood when you're standing in front of her parlor."

Bingo.

Baba's house wasn't a magical deception, it was a quirk of building. The only way to get to the normal part of the house was from the secret staircase passageway. If you came in the front, you'd never suspect there was an eldritch parlor filled with fortune telling memorabilia underneath you, through a closet door. If you came up the pathway, you'd be totally unaware that there was a builder-grade tract home a few yards away.

"Why didn't the first responders figure this out?" I asked Stormy. "You'd think they'd have a GPS that would have clued them in that the parlor was below a neighborhood. Part of a whole other house."

"Mariner's Cove is a small town and, as you've learned, most municipal positions are held by volunteers," she said. "You told them how to get here, and that's the way they came. They probably don't know that Baba is someone else. They obviously haven't swept her house for clues. They probably won't."

Stormy's phone beeped with a text alert. "It's Titanic," she said. "Diving Bill has finished his report."

Chapter Thirteen

Stormy bolted into the house, down the stairs, and through the parlor with Waggery in close pursuit, flying low behind her. I had no choice but to trail after them.

Had we closed and locked the front door? Did we leave anything behind that might implicate us in a crime? I stuffed the mystery emerald ring into my pocket, the gesture reminding me that we hadn't found mine. I couldn't think about that. The report was ready. Everything was happening too quickly and all I could do was try to keep up.

Tromping down the hidden trail was a lot easier—and faster and scarier—than going up. We were in the center of town in a few minutes. Waggery enjoyed the speed and landed contentedly on my shoulder as we pushed the door open to Titanic's office.

"This is almost as surprising as Baba's house," I said. "It's so dull in here. No decks being swabbed. No eyes being patched. What kind of a pirate is he?"

"He's a pirate with a law degree," Stormy said. *"Dread Pirate Law-Abiding Citizen."*

"Right this way, ladies." Titanic ushered us into his office and motioned for us to take a seat.

"For starters," he said, "I'm not representing you in an official capacity. This is a personal call, not anything you will be billed for."

"Does it fall under attorney-client privilege?" I asked.

"Do you need it to?"

"Um, wow," I said. "Not sure?"

"I'm joking, Carrie," he said. "Relax. If you need to confess anything, we'll discuss whether I need to represent you, but right now it's like we're hanging out at a pirate party. With a lot less rum."

"Great," I said. "What did Diving Bill find?"

"He's made an interesting ruling," he said.

"You mean it's murder?"

"What? No," said Titanic. "I find it odd that you would jump to that conclusion."

"What other option is there?" Stormy asked.

"It appears that Baba's death was an accident," Titanic said. "She choked to death."

"What did she choke on?" Stormy asked.

"That's where you come in, Carrie." Titanic said.

"Me? Why me?"

Titanic pushed a black-and-white photo across his desk. "This is what she choked on."

I picked up the photo.

"That can't be—" I said and handed the photo to Stormy.

"Carrie," she said. "That's your ring."

Waggery pecked at the photo. "No wonder you couldn't find it," I said to him. I pulled him into my lap.

"Oh, no," he said.

"Couldn't have said it better myself," I whispered.

Chapter Fourteen

I broke into a sweat—an uncommon occurrence in a place where the temperature rarely rises above fifty-five degrees.

Waggery made gagging sounds.

"Not now, buddy," I said, and he quieted down. "I'm stunned. How did this happen? I don't understand."

"It's a mystery," Titanic said. "From my point of view as an attorney, this is simply a fact. She choked on your ring. But that's all we know. It's going to take some sleuthing to figure out how she got the ring and why it was in her mouth."

Titanic leaned back in his chair. "This is uncomfortable. But if you need to speak up, Carrie, now is the time. Tell me everything you know."

"You're shivering," Stormy said. She put her arm around me.

"I—I have nothing to add." My mind raced. I could truthfully tell him I had no idea how Baba got my ring. But what about the rest? Could I tell him about our trip to Baba's and the ring in my pocket?

Stormy gave my shoulder a squeeze. "You don't know how she got the ring, do you, Carrie?"

My thoughts were so scrambled that I wasn't sure if Stormy was trying to tell me what to say or if she was simply comforting me?

"I don't know how she got it," I said, desperate to deflect. "What happens now? Do I get my ring back? Is it evidence? Am I going to be arrested? Stormy, how did this happen?"

"Not sure," she said. "Titanic, what are our next steps?"

"The report doesn't mention ownership of the ring," he said in a lawyerly tone I'd not heard before. He was taking this seriously, and I wasn't sure if that was a good thing or a bad thing. "I know that Diving Bill was there when Baba saw your ring and made a fuss. I don't know if he doesn't remember, or if he has another reason for not mentioning it."

"Wait," I said. "You think Diving Bill left the fact that I own the ring out of the report on purpose?"

"I'm not in a position to question anyone's motives," he said. "I don't know Diving Bill that well. He's only been here a short time. But so far, my dealings with him have shown that he's a good guy. Above-board. And a terrific knitter." He rubbed his scarf between his two fingers.

"What are you saying?" I asked.

"I'm suggesting he wouldn't be the kind of guy to lie about important facts. He is either not sure of the provenance of that ring, or doubts that it's yours for some reason not revealed in the report. Or he's protecting you."

"Protecting me? Why?"

"I think you need to go find out," he said. "As soon as possible."

Chapter Fifteen

Needless to say, I was shaken and confused by this turn of events, so I was glad that Stormy remembered to ask Titanic if we could keep the report.

"I'll print you a copy," he said. "Now, if you'll excuse me, I have some lawyering to do."

"I'm starving," Stormy said as we stepped out onto the sidewalk. "Let's get some grub."

"I want to go see Diving Bill," I said. "Now."

"Of course you do," Stormy said. "For one thing, I'm not sure where he is. If his report is finished, he might not be at the coroner's office. I don't think we should go drawing attention to ourselves there."

"What should we do, then?"

"Let's take the report back to my place and look for clues ourselves," she said. "We need to figure out what he knows, how he knows it, and try to untangle his thought process. I don't get why he would want to protect a person he hardly knows. And please don't be offended, but you didn't make a stellar impression."

"Hey!" I said in a mock-offended tone. "He kept getting me drinks."

"I'm not blaming you," she said. "But you did threaten to murder Baba."

"Ugh," I said. "I didn't mean it. I barely remember it."

"Unfortunately, that room was filled with people who probably do remember it."

"I'm so embarrassed," I said. "How did this happen?"

"Those rapscallions have that effect on people," she said. "Don't beat yourself up about it. We've all been there. Let's go home. I'll make omelets."

Think Ink was a few blocks down the street from Titanic's law office. I was relieved when we arrived. It had been a stressful day so far, and I was looking forward to feeding Waggery and settling down in front of the fireplace. We had a mysterious flash drive and a lot of papers to sort through, and I was eager to find anything that would help me connect these strange coincidences and mysterious motivations. I was also keen to prove I had nothing to do with any of it.

The door to Think Ink was ajar when we arrived.

"Uh-oh," I said. "I don't like the look of this."

Stormy pushed the door open slowly. "Hello?" she called out. "Who's here?"

Nothing appeared to be broken or overturned. The register was still in its position on the checkout counter. My tarot table and chairs were all upright and intact. My hand instinctively went to my pocket. I was relieved to find my tarot cards there, as they should be.

But the velvet throw pillows from Think Ink's waiting area were strewn all over the floor, from one end of the shop to the other.

"This is the weirdest break in I've ever seen," I said.

"The floor is lava, Stormy!" a boy's voice said.

"Spike, how did you get in here?"

"The door was open," he said. "You can only step on those things. The floor is lava."

Waggery flew over and landed on Stormy's stool.

"This is insane," Stormy said. "You know you can't be in here alone. It's not safe."

"That other lady was here alone."

"What lady?" Stormy asked.

"That lady with the red hair," Spike said. "I saw her through the window even though she left the lights off."

"What was she doing in here?" I asked. "Could you see?"

"I don't know. The floor was lava when I got here."

I went to the checkout counter. Nothing appeared to be missing or out of order. Stormy looked into her cabinets and drawers.

"The floor is still lava!" Spike cried in a pitch meant for dolphins before darting out of the shop.

"She was here, Stormy," I said. "The ghost."

"I don't think anything's missing," she said. "Except for Spike's lava game, it all appears—normal."

"That's because she didn't take anything," I said. I handed Stormy an envelope with her name on it. "Looks like she broke in to leave something behind."

Chapter Sixteen

Stormy put the piece of paper back in the envelope and stuffed it in her pocket.

"Can you and Waggery let yourselves in upstairs? I have to take care of this."

"You're leaving?" I couldn't believe it. "Where are you going?"

She kissed my forehead. "I'll be right back. Why don't you go upstairs, log into my laptop, and see what's on Baba's flash drive?"

She dashed out.

"The floor is lava," I called out behind her.

I put the pillows back on the sofas in the waiting area, and Waggery tossed them onto the floor again until I got stern with him.

"Stop it, Waggery," I said. "I know you think this is fun, but I'm stressed out. Plus, it's past your lunchtime."

"Oh, no," he said in Stormy's voice. He'd gotten very good at imitating her. When we arrived in Mariner's Cove, I was worried about him leaving me to live with the wizened old sea ravens; now I was worried he was starting to like Stormy better than me.

Back in the loft, I fed a grateful Waggery (and myself), and made a cup of tea. I opened Stormy's laptop. Waggery nodded off on his perch.

Her usual password, *Category5!*, didn't work. Why had she changed it? I was too tired and frustrated from the day's events to attempt to figure it out on my own.

I texted Stormy.

What's ur laptop password?

No response.

"Enough," I said. "Stormy is off doing I-don't-know-what, and that's got me freaked out."

Waggery released a tiny, avian snore.

"I need a reading," I said. I took my cards out of their silk scarf and gently shuffled through them.

I didn't like to read myself too often. I tended to impose my own wishes and preconceived notions onto my answers and, sometimes, the readings made me more confused than when I started.

But I doubted that anything could be more confusing than it already was. I closed my eyes, centered myself, and took a few deep breaths.

I pulled a card and placed it on the coffee table in front of me.

I flipped it over.

The Devil card, reversed.

The third time in two days I'd conjured this card. It was a message I couldn't ignore.

I heard Aunt Inez's voice in my head: *'Recurring cards are a warning. Ignore them at your peril.'*

The horned monster on the card held a torch and kept two people bound to him in chains. Even though I knew that this card didn't necessarily denote evil, as I sat here, alone, in Stormy's home while she was out on a suspicious errand, I couldn't help but let the emotion of the day take over.

Had I unknowingly made a deal with the devil? What did I really know about Stormy? What was I missing? What secrets were hiding here in Mariner's Cove?

And, more importantly, how would I uncover them?

Chapter Seventeen

It was true what Aunt Inez said about recurring cards: '*When a card keeps popping up, the best option is to take a deeper dive into what the card is trying to tell you. Each card in the deck has multiple meanings depending on the situation, the question, what card it appears next to or after or above. Tarot is a lifelong learning process, one that never gets boring even if the readings are murky.*' My training had prepared me for almost every pairing, occurrence, placement, reversal—everything. But in this situation, my confusion had overridden my expertise.

Fortunately, I had a trick for that.

I relaxed my shoulders and took a few more calming breaths. Then I shuffled my deck again.

I placed four stacks of cards on the table in front of me. In clockwise order, starting at the upper left, I named each stack Career, Love, Money, and Health.

The method is to flip through each stack, find the card that's been haunting you (in this case The Devil), and determine in what area of your life it belongs.

The Devil—reversed again—appeared in my love stack,

connoting a lack of confidence in my relationship. Did this mean that I didn't trust Stormy? Or did she not trust me?

I wanted to brush this off as leftovers from the way our relationship began, with each one of us accusing the other of murder. But in the back of my mind, I knew better.

I trusted Stormy.

Didn't I?

Our life together had been smooth sailing recently, but our relationship nearly crashed on the rocks before it even left shore. We'd met about six months prior, on the day her father—who was the mayor of my hometown and my close friend—was murdered. It was a confusing mess, and we each believed the other might be responsible. Thank goodness, that proved to not be the case. But after we solved the murders of both Mayor Preston Brix and his fiancée (and my friend) Emma Fort-Knightly, we found ourselves faced with more questions than answers.

My Uncle Grist revealed to us that my Aunt Inez had been involved with a secret society called Ravenous Partners before she died.

"The goal of Ravenous Partners," he explained, "was to transform our hometown of Prosperity into a top-tier travel destination."

"Aunt Inez was working with the mayor on his tourism initiatives?" I asked.

"Along with Emma and the head of tourism, Flynt Burns, and others," Grist continued. "Then things went terribly wrong."

"Wrong, how?"

"When Inez was still part of the group, she advocated for a measured, slow growth option. But, as you know, the rest of the group was greedy. They pressured her. In disturbing ways."

"What do you mean?"

"It's about your rings."

Stormy had come to Prosperity in search of her emerald ring. She knew her father had stolen it. She didn't know he'd been murdered. We solved the crime together and then found out some shocking news.

"You'd better sit down," Grist said.

Lillian, who wasn't Grist's girlfriend yet, but she was angling for it, paced nervously in the background, eyeing the ring that Grist had told me to remove from a secret compartment in my fireplace.

"We shouldn't dive into this unpleasantness now, Grist," she said. "The girls and Hank have already been through so much. It's all in the past."

Grist considered what she said.

"You're right," he said. "It was an ugly time. And it's over now. The rings are your keepsakes now."

"Why do Stormy and I have matching rings?" It was the only question I could force out of my mouth, but certainly not the only one (that) I had.

"We should eat," Lillian said. "The food's getting cold."

Grist glanced at her quickly. She sat down.

Grist looked pained, but he continued. "Our work with Ravenous Partners resulted in a lot of good. Prosperity is flourishing. But, as you recently saw, greed got the better of some of us. These rings were a part of that—a part I have no desire to revisit other than to make sure yours is safely in your possession. Always."

"Grist," Stormy said. "Couldn't selling the ring help Carrie? I don't mean to speak for her, but she was worried her belongings were being repossessed not that long ago."

Grist interrupted by letting out a long sigh. "This ring is priceless. I would never let her sell it. Impossible."

"I'd never want to," I said, putting it on the ring finger of my right hand. "Stormy and I match."

"The sweetest outcome any of us could've hoped for," Lillian said. "Now, please, eat. My love language is food."

"I want one, too," Hank said, getting up to go to the table. "That emerald would look gorgeous with my red hair."

"Shut up, Hank," Stormy said. She punched him in the arm. I knew not to intervene in their bickering. Hank had kidnapped Stormy and tied her up in a secret tunnel, and I could understand why she wasn't ready to let that go. She seemed a little softer toward him, though. She didn't use a knuckle when she punched him anymore.

In the warmth of this scene, Stormy and I had somehow forgotten to address the questions that would shape the next few weeks of our life together: Why did we have these rings? Where did they come from? And were they worth dying for?

I put the cards back into their scarf, vowing to go through them in detail later. I had hoped for clarity, but, as usual, I found myself more befuddled than ever.

Where was Stormy? What was in that envelope? I hoped it was a thank you note from Spike or an invitation to a party she wanted to surprise me with. But sitting here, stewing, was doing me no good.

And people didn't normally break into a building to leave a note if the note had good news.

"Waggery," I said, standing up. "I need to go out. You need to be a good boy."

Lucky for me, he was sound asleep on his perch.

I wanted my ring back. And I knew exactly where it was.

Chapter Eighteen

The town of Mariner's Cove was smaller and more densely packed than Prosperity. I loved the cloak-and-dagger feel of creeping through narrow, dimly lit alleyways. The perpetual mist gave everything a gloomy mood, and if I'd had the right clothing for the weather, I would've appreciated the cool stillness of this place.

My teeth were chattering by the time I got to the coroner's office, but I was undeterred.

However, there was one small problem.

"I'm here to see Diving Bill," I said to the lady behind the desk.

"I'm sorry, ma'am. Who?" The receptionist was cautious. I could sense that she was used to accommodating unusual personalities. There was no way she could know that the person standing in front of her in a cotton dress and no coat was sane.

I was sane. Wasn't I?

"I'm sorry," I said. "The coroner."

"Do you have an appointment?"

"Do people need to have an appointment? Seems like the kind of job that requires a healthy acceptance of spontaneity."

She looked at me blankly.

"He has something that belongs to me," I said. "I'm wondering if it's possible to get it back."

"His name is William Fitzwilliam, for future reference."

"Oh, fancy," I said.

"Your name, please?"

"Carrie Fitzcarrie."

Once again, she stared blankly.

"Sorry, I'm nervous," I said. "Trying to make a joke. Carrie Dettwiler."

She picked up the phone. "Mr. Fitzwilliam? Carrie Dettwiler is here to see you." She hung up. "You can go on back."

The door buzzed, and I pushed through into a narrow hallway. Diving Bill stood at the end of the hall, as if he'd been waiting to greet me.

"Carrie! To what do I owe the pleasure?" He motioned for me to have a seat once we got into his office.

"Nice sweater," I said. He was wearing the chunkiest, coziest fisherman's sweater I'd ever seen. I assumed he'd knitted it himself. "It's like a blanket with sleeves."

"Ah, thank you!" he said. "I've started a scarf for you." He opened a desk drawer and pulled out a few rows of moss green yarn, perfectly knit. "From the looks of things, you need it. It's not done yet, obviously. I don't think you could even use it as a potholder at this stage."

"I'm freezing here," I said. "That's beautiful. And so thoughtful. When I get back to Prosperity, I'll take it with me to my favorite thrift store to find a coat that matches."

"Prosperity?"

"Have you been there?" I asked.

"I have," he said. "Lovely place. Nice people."

"All true," I said.

"You didn't come down here to discuss your hometown. How can I help you?"

"I saw the report," I said. "The object that choked Baba. I think it belongs to me."

He leaned into his desk, his hands in a triangle. "This is highly unusual."

"I understand," I said. "It's an important heirloom given to me, sort of, by my Aunt Inez. Stormy has a matching one."

He looked surprised. "What do you mean 'sort of'?"

"I know it sounds weird. I can explain it all over a glass of mead at a future pirate party, but for now I need to know how I can get my ring back."

"Baba's death appears to be a tragic accident," he said. "It is concerning that she choked to death on your property."

He took the scarf he said he was making for me out of the drawer and started knitting.

"Helps me think," he said. "Did you give it to Baba? The ring?"

I needed to be careful about what I shared with Diving Bill. He couldn't know that Stormy and I had been snooping around Baba's house earlier that same day. And my first theory—that the gray lady had stolen my ring—seemed too simple. If she had, Baba choked on my ring while I slept on her porch. I couldn't fathom that series of events. I leaned into the chaos of the pirate party.

"You were there," I said. "Remember? She burst into Think Ink, raised a ruckus, looked at my ring, and swanned off. Baba got the ring off my finger."

"How? In front of all those people?"

"She's a fortune teller," I said, shrugging. "They have all kinds of ways of getting your money."

"Do you do that?"

"Do what? Tell fortunes?"

Diving Bill nodded and seemed a little more interested than I was comfortable with.

"Absolutely not," I said. "I'm a tarot card reader. Not a fortune teller. There's a difference. I went to Stanford."

The fancy college connection wasn't something I used to impress others, but I wanted to deflect his attention as much as possible.

"Well, Ms. Dettwiler," he said. "I think the best thing for us to focus on is getting your ring back to you efficiently and expeditiously. Let me make sure I cross my Ts and dot my Is to ensure that it can be released to you legally and with no encumbrances or legal problems. You'll have to prove it's yours, of course."

My head swam. "I don't know how to do that."

"Give it some thought. Maybe a family member can provide documentation? There's no rush. It's safe here in this building. But I'll call you with the procedures you need to follow and the documents you'll need to prove ownership, and we'll go from there."

My eyes filled with tears. I would be leaving his office without my ring.

"Oh, Carrie," he said. "It's going to be fine. This is distressing, but you will get your ring back." He handed me a tissue.

"It's very important to me," I said. "It's an heirloom."

"I understand," he said. "Try to see things from my point of view."

"Your point of view?"

"I signed my name to the report and my word is as good as gold. But I do wonder—"

"Wonder what?" I asked through tears.

"Why she had this accident with your property," he said. "It raises some questions." He scribbled a note on a small piece of paper.

His tone let me know that the less information I gave him, the better. I only wanted one thing—my ring.

"I don't want to make any assumptions," he said. "I'm certainly not accusing you of anything. For good measure, you may want to have a chat with Titanic."

"Why?" I asked. "I mean, I love talking with him, but why?"

"Because I think you need a lawyer."

Chapter Nineteen

A quick shortcut through an alley and a right turn onto a cobblestone street, and I was in front of Titanic's law office. Mariner's Cove's streetlights were flickering on, giving the scene a touch of romantic light.

Titanic was locking up.

"You're back," he said. "If we keep meeting like this, people will talk."

"That's the last thing I need."

"What's wrong?"

Titanic's gigantic presence, like a helpful Sasquatch, made me feel safe. So safe that I spilled everything about my conversation with Diving Bill, the origin of my ring, why Stormy had a matching one, and the requirements for getting my own ring back.

I didn't mention that I had found a similar, yet smaller, ring at Baba's house, and that it was currently in my pocket. Keeping these things to myself, despite how warm and comforting Titanic was being, seemed like the right thing to do. In the past, I'd always told everyone everything with very little prompting. Perhaps this was a sign of maturity, that I was able to hold some information back until I was one-hundred percent certain the other person was trustworthy. Or it was a huge red flag that I was turning into a sneaky sneaker who bends the truth to save her own butt.

The jury was still out.

"You're shivering," he said. "Let's get you home."

A good idea. Unloading all of this onto Titanic made me feel deflated, exhausted.

We climbed the stairs to Stormy's residence. Waggery immediately flew to Titanic's shoulder.

"Look at that," I said. "He likes you."

"This little matey's a swashy at heart," he said. "Either that or he thinks I'm a tree."

"Or a crow's nest," I said, allowing myself to break my cardinal rule of never alluding to crows when talking about my raven. I don't have a problem with crows, but ravens—my raven in particular—are special.

"*Arrggh*," Waggery said, in a dead ringer for Titanic's voice.

We flopped onto Stormy's sofa.

"It sounds like all you need," he began, "is a certificate, statement, or receipt that proves the ring is yours. My experience with expensive jewelry, especially antiques, is that documentation accompanies every purchase. People don't spend thousands of dollars on a piece of antique jewelry if they don't have proof of its provenance. Do you not have that?"

"I pulled the ring out of a fireplace," I said.

"Excuse me?" he said.

"It was my own fireplace, and my Uncle Grist told me where it was hidden," I said. "I pulled it out of a hidden compartment. Stormy was there. She can vouch for me."

"Was there anyone else there when you—let me make sure I got this right—you pulled a very expensive, very old emerald ring, exactly like the one your girlfriend has, out of a fireplace?"

From the tone of his voice, I could tell this would be a bad time to confess that I had Baba's ring in my pocket.

"Yes," I said. "Uncle Grist, his now-wife Lillian, my childhood friend Hank, and Waggery were there."

"This extraction from the fireplace occurred on your property?" he asked.

"Yes."

"That might be enough, legally, to prove that it's yours," he said. "In place of the papers, in case we don't find them, can you get any of them to validate your claim?"

"Grist and Lillian are on their honeymoon," I said. "They won't be back for several weeks. Hank has responsibilities in Prosperity, but it's possible I could get him to come here for a day or two. Pretty sure Stormy's on my team. And Waggery? Totally untrustworthy, so I don't think he'll be any help."

Waggery giggled.

"Of course," Titanic said, ignoring my joke. "Don't worry about this now. I'll help you in any way I can to gather the proof. When Stormy returns, I suggest you have dinner and a quiet evening at home. Getting worked up about this helps no one. You've already been through a lot."

"True," I said. My thoughts immediately went to the flash drive. I had plenty of things to occupy myself with this evening. Getting under a blanket, for starters.

Titanic stood up.

"Now, if you'll excuse me, I'm gonna steal her laser gun so that she can't win the next round of Assassin."

"I'm not sure I can let you do that," I said. "I'm not exactly neutral. Especially now that I need her to put in a good word for me with the town coroner-slash-pirate-slash-knitting-maven."

"You're not going to need her because we'll get the papers." He was rifling through Stormy's kitchen cabinets. "You'll thank me later. She's deadly. You don't want her to go on a rampage, do you? Slaughter all your new friends?"

"I'll show you where she keeps it."

As I was opening the drawer where I suspected Stormy had stashed her faux gun, my phone rang.

It was Bill. I answered.

"That was fast," I said. "I'm so glad you got back to me. I want to get this resolved as quickly as possible."

"We all do," Diving Bill said.

"Can I come by tomorrow to pick up my ring?"

"Only if you have the paperwork. I double checked with the authorities. The bad news is that the state requires documentation before I can release it."

My heart sank. "Tell me exactly what you need from me for proof, and I'll do whatever it takes to get it to you." I was pricklier than I wanted to be, annoyed that he saw the ring on me with his own eyes yet refused to make an exception. But then I remembered what Aunt Inez would say to me when the world was against me.

'*You're special*. Just *like everyone else*.'

I relaxed and decided to do exactly what he asked. No complaining. Show up with the paperwork like a grownup and retrieve my property legally and above board. Even if it might take a while.

Titanic swept his hands along the tops of her cabinets. He didn't even have to stand on his tiptoes.

Diving Bill continued. "You should have the original bill of sale, whether it was bought through a private dealer or auction, the appraisal, and the inventory number if it is from a museum or private collection. No copies. All documents must be original, and the signatures must be legible."

"Is that all?" I hoped the sarcasm didn't come through. I was trying so hard to fight it. "There's a complicated history with these rings. I don't know if it's possible." My head throbbed.

"Rings?" he said. "I'm not sure I understand."

"It doesn't matter," I said, chiding myself for revealing that there were more rings in play. I wanted to keep this transaction as simple as possible.

"Carrie?" Titanic was trying to get my attention.

"Look, Bill, this is bad news," I said.

"It seems that way," he said.

Titanic waved to get my attention as Diving Bill continued to chatter in my ear. "

I mouthed *what*.

He mouthed *hang up the phone*.

When a seven-foot man tells you to hang up, you hang up.

"I have to go," I said to Bill. I ended the call. "What is it, Titanic?"

"I think you need to see this," he said. He showed me Stormy's fake gun.

I felt a squeeze of annoyance. Did he think his Assassin game was more important than attempting to reclaim a highly valuable, possibly priceless, personal heirloom?

"I think you should take it if you want to win the next round of Assassin," I said. "Don't worry, your secret's safe with me."

"It's not that," he said. "When we play Assassin, we use these cheap plastic things Scurvy Doug found on the internet. You push the trigger, which is a little button, and a laser shines on the target. It's silly, but it's fun and it works. Once you've been hit, there's no denying. And no one gets hurt."

"What's the problem?" I asked. "Is it that she'll probably order another online and destroy you all, anyway?"

"No," Titanic said. "She can do that. But the problem with this one is that it's not a laser gun at all. It's real."

Chapter Twenty

The floor lurched and the room wobbled. The stress of the day's events, combined with the discovery of a firearm in Stormy's home, made me woozy. What had started out as a couple of fun weeks with my cute girlfriend in her picturesque town was turning into a chaotic, violent sideshow. Where was Stormy? She needed to answer for this.

"Oh, no," Waggery said, sensing my mood.

"Do you know why Stormy would have a firearm?" Titanic asked, placing it on the counter, its barrel conspicuously pointing away from us. He crossed his arms as if he expected me to explain it all.

"Of course not," I said, my voice edged with irritation. "I have never had a reason to carry a gun, and I'm not going to start now. And if Stormy thinks having an unsecured gun in the house without telling me is acceptable, well, that's an argument we're going to need to have. What if Waggery got hold of it? Or Spike?"

"I wasn't accusing you," he said in a calm and measured tone. "I'm only asking."

I took a breath and remembered that Titanic didn't know

me. If he wasn't aware of Stormy's gun prior to my arrival, he could easily jump to the conclusion that I was somehow involved in purchasing a firearm. If there's anything I've learned about people from the past few months, it's that you can't judge people by how they look. I may be sunshine to Stormy's grumpy, but Titanic had no way of knowing that I despised guns.

"I'm as eager for an answer as you are," I said. My chest tightened. What did this mean?

I was sure Stormy had the gun for protection.

I had to be sure, because my next thought was that she planned to use it on me. I pushed that theory aside. Impossible. We were in love.

Weren't we?

"You don't know where she went?"

"I don't," I said. "We came back here. The shop door was open. Spike was there. I found an envelope with her name on it. She read what was inside and then she ran out. That was hours ago."

Titanic paced for a few seconds, rubbing his chin. "What did Bill tell you?"

"He provided a list of all the documents I'll need to prove it's my ring," I said. "He might as well have told me I need to find a map on the back of the United States constitution."

I laughed at the absurdity of it.

Waggery giggled.

Titanic processed this information.

"Carrie, your visit to Mariner's Cove has been one for the record books," he said, not looking at me.

"Thank you, Titanic," I said. "All I wanted was to visit my girlfriend, read some cards, and make some money. I didn't ask for any of this."

"Grab your coat." He walked to the door. "Or a sweater."

I eyed the fireplace and the faux fur rug on Stormy's soft leather sofa.

"I don't have the energy," I said. "I can't go anywhere."

"I insist." He offered me his plate-sized hand. "We're going to get you some seafood stew."

When hurricane Titanic sweeps you up in his bluster, it's impossible to resist. I gave Waggery a small snack, kissed him on his beak, and told him to be a good boy. Within a few minutes, I was being squired through Mariners Cove's labyrinthine streets to a restaurant called Down the Hatch.

"What if Stormy comes home and I'm not there?" I asked as I slid into a wide, comfy booth.

"She can call you," he said. "Besides, she left you and Waggery alone there, didn't she?"

"I don't want to get into one of these 'you did this to me, so I'm doing this to you' situations in our relationship. That's not sustainable."

"Very healthy," he said. "If she has a problem with it, I'll verify that I didn't give you a choice. You need to eat. And Barnacle Brandon makes the best seafood stew you'll ever eat."

"Barnacle Brandon?"

"He was with us the other night, but you might not remember," he said. "There's your drinking buddy, Scurvy Doug. Give him a little wave. He's working the bar."

I made eye contact with Scurvy Doug and gave a half-hearted wave.

"Don't remind me," I said. "So embarrassing."

"Nah," he said. "Not for you. You were powerless against a troop of buccaneers armed with rum. But Scurvy Doug?" He lowered his voice and looked around. "The rest of the marauders are worried about him."

"Oh?"

"It's become a pattern. A bit of a blackout drinker. Don't say anything to him, but we're planning an intervention."

"That's serious."

"Yeah," he said. "I don't want you to think he's a bad guy because he's not. He's struggling and we want to help."

"Is there anything I can do?"

"How about you enjoy your stew?" Titanic waved over Barnacle Brandon, whom I vaguely recollected as much as I could, considering everyone at the party was a blur. Barnacle Brandon was polite but seemed busy; yet within a few minutes, I was tucking into the richest, spiciest, most filling stew I'd ever tasted.

"You were right," I said. "This is hitting the spot."

Titanic was already done and signaling to Brandon for another bowl. "Big guy," he said.

I nodded. "No judgment here." The stew was working its magic, warming me from the inside out. I was snug and cozy, like I was in the hull of a wooden ship. A very fancy wooden ship, with excellent service, candlelight, cloth napkins and a giant who I secretly hoped would pick up the check.

"It's been a long time since I've been out to a nice restaurant," I said. "Thank you for bringing me here. After everything that's happened, I didn't know how much I needed it."

"I want you to feel welcome in Mariner's Cove," he said. "You've had a rough go. But I need to tell you something. Now that we're friends."

"Anything," I said. The stew was so filling and the ambiance so relaxing that I'd almost forgotten the drama of the past few days.

"Don't let your guard down," he said. "With Stormy."

I sat up a little straighter. "What do you mean? Do you know what's going on with her?"

"Unfortunately, I think I do," he said. "You're not going to like it."

"I already don't like it," I said. "If there's anything I have learned lately, not knowing the truth doesn't make bad feelings better."

"Did Stormy ever tell you about her last girlfriend?"

"A little," I said. "She was a meter maid. A bit stalky. Didn't take the break-up well."

"All of that is true," he said. "There's one more thing."

"Yes?"

"She was a redhead."

A light breeze would have knocked me down.

"Do you think this gray ghost is Stormy's ex? And that Stormy's been leaving me here to meet up with her? Is that what you're saying, Titanic? Do you think the gun has anything to do with her behavior?"

"I don't know, Carrie," he said. "Everybody loves Stormy. And I hate to cause friction where there is none. But her love life has been messy. Real messy."

"Do you think this be-cloaked ginger is going to harm me in some way?" I was feeling ungenerous and emphasized the word 'ginger' as if it were a slur. As if my best friend in Prosperity, Hank, didn't look exactly like Prince Harry. I was uncomfortable with the jealous side of me and frustrated with Stormy for behaving so suspiciously.

"My best advice to you is to talk to her about it," he said. "Call her to the carpet. She's a good person who had a difficult upbringing. You know about her dad and all?"

"Boy, do I," I said, without elaborating.

"She doesn't trust easily, so she believes she's untrustworthy. That's why she sneaks around. Most of the time, she's not up to anything bad. It's the way she goes about things that makes her seem...questionable."

"You've given me food, and now you've given me food for thought, Titanic Jones," I said. "Thank you."

"I think you're good for her," he said. "I want nothing more than for Stormy to find happiness. Oh, gosh, wait a sec."

He pulled his phone from his pocket.

"She's not—. Hang on. Oh, man. Okay. Look, we'll take this up another time. I gotta run."

"But—"

"I'll tell Barnacle Brandon to put this on my tab," he said. "I'm so sorry. Stay as long as you'd like and get whatever you want. We'll finish this another time."

"Wait—"

I watched Titanic leave.

"Wow," I said to no one. I pulled out my phone. Nothing from Stormy. What was happening? I decided to finish my stew and head home. I missed Waggery and was a little worried he might have upended Stormy's garbage or torn up her sofa pillows.

"Hullo, again."

I looked up to see Scurvy Doug standing next to my booth with his hands in his pockets and a sheepish expression on his face.

"Hi, there," I said. "Good to see you. Have a seat."

He looked nervous, shaky, but didn't sit. "I wanted to apologize," he said. "To you."

"You don't owe me an apology," I said. "At all. I was happy to meet you and I'm happy to be here with you now. You look uncomfortable. Would you like some stew?"

"Oh, no," he said, shivering. "I wanted to say I'm sorry. For everything."

"Doug. Or is it Scurvy?" I smiled at my own joke. "You have nothing to apologize for."

"I think I might," he said, unable to meet my gaze. "Can I—can I come see you tomorrow? For a reading?"

"Of course," I said. "What time?"

"I'll be there at nine," he said. "Will that work?"

"Yes. You're in the calendar." I pretended to add him into my phone as if I had a busy schedule—a meek attempt to lighten the mood. I was delighted to schedule a reading, but Doug looked so haunted that I didn't want him to think I was happy about his distress.

"I'm looking forward to getting to know you better," I said.

"I need to get to the bottom of something," he said. "And I think you might be the only person who can help me."

Chapter Twenty-One

Scurvy Doug was on my mind as I walked back to Stormy's alone. Would I be limited in how I could help? I steeled myself for the possibility that his tarot reading could be difficult. There were limits to what I could do (as a tarot card reader). I could reveal new ways of viewing his situation, or I could illuminate opportunities that he may have overlooked. But I couldn't get him healthy. Or convince him to make different choices.

Aunt Inez used to say, *'You can lead a client to water, but you can't make them think'*. I had a responsibility to give an honest reading and to offer a fair opinion about what I saw, if asked. Unfortunately, I wasn't a trained psychologist or even a life coach. What the client did with the insights they paid me for was completely up to them.

Nevertheless, I was worried about him.

"Where have you been?"

Stormy and Waggery were on the sofa. Waggery was giving her kisses.

"Mwah," he said. "Mwah. Mwah."

"I could ask the same of you," I said. "I was having stew with Titanic. And booking a reading with Scurvy Doug tomorrow."

"Oh, man," she said. "That should be interesting. He's got some issues."

"Are we going to pretend that you didn't abandon me for the last several hours? Why did you ignore my text?"

"My phone died," she said, pointing to the place on the kitchen counter where it was plugged into the wall. "What did you need?"

"What did I 'need'? Are you joking? I *needed* your password so that I could get into that flash drive. I *needed* you alongside me when I went to see Diving Bill about getting my ring back. But I also *need* to understand why my girlfriend got a mysterious note after her shop was broken into and then disappeared for hours."

"I had some old, boring business to take care of," she said. "It's over now. No big whoop. Everything's fine."

"Is it?" I asked, walking toward the kitchen. I pulled out her gun, careful not to point it at her. It was heavier than I thought it would be. Holding it felt obscene. "What's this for?"

"You should probably put that down. I don't think it's loaded—"

"You don't think?" I put it down and backed away.

"Who was snooping? And why?"

"No one was snooping," I said. "Titanic wanted to play a prank on you, and he found this instead. Why do you have a firearm? Parking tickets again?"

I didn't like my own tone. I'd been hard on Stormy once before, when we were running all over Prosperity trying to clear our names from her father's—and then Emma Fort-Knightly's— murder. But that was before I knew her. Stormy could come across as guarded, but I no longer doubted her inherent *goodness*. My demanding attitude conveyed none of that.

"The gun was given to me by someone," she said, very slowly, probably trying not to spook me any more than I already was. "It's not loaded, and it never has been. I was only joking about that. I don't even have bullets. It's been on top of my cabinets since I received it because I don't know how to get rid of a firearm legally."

"Why would someone give you a gun, Stormy?"

"For protection," she said. "I was in a bit of trouble once and a friend made the very misguided attempt to show concern. That's all."

"I don't like guns," I said. "I don't like that I don't know where you were this evening. I'm up to here with secrets, ugly discoveries, and bad news."

She got up off the couch and approached me. "I agree," she said. "My disappearance tonight was unacceptable. But it was necessary."

"Where were you?"

"Does it matter? It's over," she said. "I'm sorry I hurt you, and I promise I'll never abandon you like that again. I didn't think it would take so long. I didn't think that my phone battery would die. Carrie, I'm—I'm so sorry."

Exhaustion was pulling me under. "I don't have the energy for this, Stormy. I can't leave Mariner's Cove, especially now. I can't afford a hotel, and what quaint, luxuriously priced bed-and-breakfast will take a raven? I need you to be honest and transparent from here on out. No weird running off. No lies. Answer your phone. And get rid of this gun."

"I swear," she said, holding up two fingers like a Boy Scout. "How about this? We spend the rest of the evening seeing what we can learn about Baba and figuring out how to get your ring back. Tomorrow, after your appointment with Scurvy Doug, I'll take you and Waggery out to The Shipwrecks. And we'll toss the gun in the sea."

I wanted to believe her.

I did believe her.

Whether my trust in Stormy would work out in the long run remained to be seen. But I was ready to put this behind me and start looking to the future—and the future was on Baba's flash drive.

"That sounds like a plan," I said. "Now, what's your password? I've got some more snooping to do."

"It's '*stormy+carrie4eva!*'"

"No, it's not!"

She handed me her laptop. "Go ahead," she said. "Try it."

I typed it and I was in.

Chapter Twenty-Two

Stormy was full of surprises. When we booted up her laptop, I discovered that her background image was a photo of my cottage.

"This is not what I would imagine Stormy Portwood would have on home screen."

"Look around," she said. "I love Mariner's Cove, but even a dark spirit such as myself needs sunshine every now and then."

I smiled at the image, roses abloom, hollyhocks bending in the breeze. I could see the faint outline of Waggery in the window. I pulled Stormy's throw blanket around me and allowed myself to feel homesick. Even though Prosperity was only forty miles away, the weather made me feel as if I'd traveled halfway around the world.

Stormy popped the flash drive in. It was unnamed.

"You'd think she'd have named it *Here There Be Hexes* or *Fortune Favors the Files*, Stormy said. "Colorful woman. Boring flash drive."

"She was living a double life as a bland suburbanite," I said. "Maybe that side of her personality did all of her filing and computer work."

"Good point," Stormy said. "When you saw Diving Bill, did you mention what we had found?"

"Absolutely not. I went there to get my ring, not to confess to breaking and entering a potential crime scene."

"Good point," Stormy said. "Okay, let's see what we can learn."

She clicked open the drive to reveal a few folders: receipts, invoices, bills of sale, certificates of authenticity.

"Interesting," I said.

"Why? Seems straightforward."

"These are the kinds of documents that Diving Bill wanted me to find in order for him to hand over the ring."

"Diving Bill is being a bureaucratic knob," she said. "It's obviously yours. He was there when she took it."

"I'm not totally sure she swiped it," I said. "I remember having it on the next day when I went to her house. I think."

"Your memory may be a bit—faulty," she said. "Anyway, there were a bunch of other people in attendance who can vouch for you." She twisted her own ring on her finger, an act that seemed to me equal parts anxious and possessive. She'd been through a lot of turmoil to get her ring back, so I understood her feelings.

"Try to see it from his point of view," I said. "He has no real proof it's mine. What if someone else came in and made the same claim? He's required to ask for documentation. Besides, I didn't mention there's another one almost exactly like ours. In my pocket. This situation gets weirder and weirder."

"I don't know what I'd do if I had to prove my ring was mine," she said. "Carrie, I'm sorry. We'll get it back."

"Thanks," I said. "I probably can't do anything until Grist and Lillian return from their honeymoon. Grist will know where to find this information if it exists. In the meantime, let's dig through Baba's files."

We opened each file and read Baba's administrative records.

"This is odd," I said, looking at an invoice for a collection of tea leaf-reading cups and saucers. "I saw a bill of sale for these over here—" I opened the file I remembered. "She bought them for a lot less than she sold them for."

"That's typical, isn't it?" Stormy asked. "Buy low, sell high."

"It is," I said. "For a dealer. Hear me out. I have a feeling Baba wasn't really a fortune teller. I think she was an antiques dealer who specialized in fortune telling curiosities. Remember how I said divination is a hard business? And how it's strange none of you knew her? She didn't advertise. She only had one sign, and it was on a fence on a deer path that no one really sees or notices. It's bizarre."

"Right," she said. "Especially when you know how extra she could be."

"What if Baba didn't tell fortunes at all—or rarely, or as more of a novelty? What if she bought and sold fortune telling memorabilia as her main source of income?"

"I don't know what difference her occupation would make," Stormy said. "Because I don't see how any of this information ties together."

"I don't either. Yet," I said. "I could be wrong. But I've seen a lot of these types of invoices and records with what Grist does with his antique wine memorabilia. I'm getting the same vibes."

"Let's keep looking," she said. "I would like to go to bed with more answers than questions at least one night in my life."

"Here," I said. "The company name is Baba Caracatiţă, but the person the bills of sale are made out to is T. Cascada."

"Do you think that's Baba's real name? Or her accountant?"

"Looks like we're going to have to find out," I said. I had opened one of the Certificates of Authenticity and found something familiar. "Does this name ring a bell?"

Stormy leaned in to get a better look. "Who is it?"

"It's LeMarcus Green," I said. "The same man who unknowingly told me on the phone a few months ago about the items Grist had secured for the wine museum. How those were fakes."

"Grist knows him!"

"Oh, he definitely does," I said. "I'm calling LeMarcus first thing in the morning."

"To ask him what?" Stormy asked.

"I'm going to ask him who Baba Caracatiţă really is. And why she stole my ring."

Chapter Twenty-Three

Both Stormy and I were dying to scour Diving Bill's report, but exhaustion overtook us, and we nodded off on the sofa. I woke up well-rested and sharp. Stormy drooled on her pillow. I fed Waggery his breakfast and took him out for a morning stroll through town.

Walks had always been part of our morning routine, and I looked forward to them as much as Waggery did. In Prosperity, I'd head straight to the town plaza, where I'd usually find my Uncle Grist leading a historical tour dressed in the full period costume of our town founder, Agustus Hoggarty. We'd also swing by the duck pond, a signature location in Prosperity (and the subject of some strange controversy, since resolved). Both Waggery and I had learned to love our time out and about, chatting with people I've known since I was a kid, and hearing jokes about ravens, crows, blackbirds, and Edgar Allan Poe in varying degrees of cleverness.

We didn't know many people here, so I didn't expect to run into friends or acquaintances. Waggery was increasingly captivated with the sea ravens, and he began to vocalize to them. But, like a stranger in a strange land, he hadn't yet learned the right words or accent. They showed a passing interest in him, but always returned to their own families and friends, like you would if you saw a person from another country in your home-town. You'd be welcoming, curious. But when you realized you couldn't communicate—and you knew the person was well cared for and looked after by their travel buddies—you'd politely move on.

I missed Prosperity, but I was grateful for this quiet time.

I had a lot of information to process, and it was nice to wander the quiet streets before they became shoulder-to-elbow with tourists. The town was similar to Prosperity, but with a doleful mist hanging in the air. This wasn't unpleasant. Mariner's Cove had been, for decades, a refreshing destination for countless thousands of overheated refugees from the Inland and Central Valleys, where summer temps often spiked to one-fifteen or higher. Here, the murky weather was touted as a feature, not a bug.

The ramshackle buildings and hidden alleyways, many of which had plaques on them denoting one historical event or another—a prominent smuggler was apprehended in the lobby of a hotel, a knife fight between two brawling brothers over the ownership rights to a lucrative trapping permit that took place right behind Down the Hatch—made me miss Grist. I knew in my bones he'd fall in love with Mariner's Cove, and I could vividly imagine him standing on a corner, dressed in period trapper garb, offering historic walking tours like he did in Prosperity.

I was so taken with my own reverie I barely registered the swish of gray wool around the corner ahead of me.

I found it hard to believe the ghost was out for a morning amble. She was the only other person I'd seen so far. I couldn't assume her appearance was a coincidence and instead decided to investigate why this mysterious person popped up everywhere I was.

"We're going to have to pick up the pace, Waggery," I said. "Hold on."

He did as he was told, and I winced from the pinch of his sharp claws. Even after several years of carting him around on my shoulder, I'd never gotten accustomed to the scratches and small punctures. I'd have scars my whole life because of my need to take Waggery everywhere I went.

I used the physical discomfort as encouragement to catch up with the gray ghost as quickly as possible. She ducked into an alley, and I followed, only to lose her, catch a glimpse of her, and lose her again around the many alleys and hidden grottoes. By the time I decided I'd lost her for good, I was so turned around I feared I wouldn't be able to find my way back to Stormy's in time to get ready to meet with Scurvy Doug.

"Whoever she is, she knows her way around Mariner's Cove," I told Waggery, who seemed to be in an elevated energetic state because of the running and confusion.

"Quok!" he cried. This was neither helpful nor comforting, but I appreciated the effort.

I couldn't wait to get Stormy's take on things. Two things were clear: this woman was observing me, and she knew the area. What I needed to get to the bottom of now was who she was and what she thought she would learn by trailing me around town.

Once again, I was alone, lost, and wondering why Stormy and her friends, who were woven into the fabric of this small town, couldn't come up with any information about a local redhead who dressed like an 18th-century sea widow? Was this because of some clever skills on the part of the gray ghost? And if so, what was she hiding? Or was she someone they all knew, and they were lying to me?

Was she Stormy's ex-girlfriend? Could it be so simple?

I wasn't sure, but I had a bad feeling about all of it.

Chapter Twenty-Four

As desperately as I wanted to fling open every back door and check under every tarp and dumpster in the backstreets of Mariner's Cove to unearth this mysterious stranger, I had a reading scheduled with Scurvy Doug, and I didn't want to be late. Waggery needed a post-walk nosh, and I needed a shower.

"I want to catch the gray lady," I said to Waggery. "When I do, the first thing I'm going to ask her is where I can get a wooly cloak like hers. My Prosperity wardrobe isn't cutting it."

Waggery shivered in solidarity.

"You're a good friend," I said. "Let's get you home."

I didn't recognize any of the businesses around me, nor the street names (where exactly would Slithery Eel Lane take me?), but I did possess the good sense to head toward the ocean. Shipwreck Rock Road ran north-south along the shore. If I headed south, I would eventually get back to the little live/work hub of artist lofts, boutiques, and bistros where Stormy lived.

She wasn't in her studio yet when I returned, so I went upstairs, fully expecting to see her at the table, sipping a cup of coffee and scrolling through her social media.

"Stormy?"

No answer. I found a sticky note on the kitchen counter:

Had to run out. Nothing to worry about. Back soon. Text me if you need anything. 💀💀💀

She put a skull-and-crossbones where the heart would have been—her own personal flourish, and frankly, a more authentic gesture for her than Xs and Os.

Waggery flew to his perch and groomed himself while I mixed some fruit into peanut butter and put it into his cup.

I showered, put on the warmest sweater I could find, and headed downstairs with my tarot deck to prepare for Scurvy Doug.

I liked to center myself with deep breathing and quiet meditation before a client arrived. People believe they're tapping into universal energies or channeling spirits. I'm not one to say whether paranormal activities are happening, and not because I'm trying to be secretive or mysterious. I honestly don't know. What I know for sure is my clients pay me money to complete a job for them, and it's my responsibility to give them the best and most accurate reading I can. Is there a spiritual component to what I offer? It's possible. I was trained by the very best, and she always said, *'how you do anything is how you do everything.'* That's why I always showed up prepared—for everything.

And so did Scurvy Doug. He arrived right on time.

When he came in, I got a clear Five of Cups vibe from him. I usually categorized my clients with a major arcana card or at least one of the court cards—Knights, Queens, etc. It makes sense to give a client a more exalted significator to help them feel important, secure. I believed the same about Scurvy Doug, of course. But the energy he was throwing off—defeated, despairing, trapped—would have been captured perfectly by a card with an image of a sorrowful person draped in a heavy cloak, turning away from upright living, and facing spilled goblets. I quietly hoped this reading would help him shake off his pain, help him see he still has support, so he could move forward. And then I could see him as a Knight or King, or even an Ace.

"Where's your friend?" he asked as he closed the door behind him.

"Stormy? Not sure. You in the market for an early-morning tattoo?"

"I meant your raven. What was his name? Wiggles?"

"It's nice of you to remember Waggery," I said, emphasizing the correct pronunciation. "I usually bring him to readings, but we had a vigorous walk this morning. I left him upstairs to rest."

I motioned for Scurvy Doug to sit down, and he did. "You took your raven for a walk?"

"Every morning," I said, handing him the cards. "He needs a lot of stimulation. If he gets bored, he gets destructive."

"So do I," Scurvy Doug said. "I get real destructive when I don't have enough—what did you call it—stimulation."

"There seems to be plenty to keep a person occupied here in Mariner's Cove," I said. "Or at least everyone seems to have multiple jobs."

"True," he said. "I do the pirating thing and I'm a bartender, as you know. But I'm also the town dogcatcher."

"Wow," I said. "Is there a big need for dogcatchers here in Mariner's Cove?"

"There is when you have as many rescue dogs as I have, which is about a dozen. My dogs are the only ones who ever get loose, so rather than getting fined every time someone called animal control on one of my loose Labradors or running Rottweilers, I volunteered to be the town dogcatcher. free of charge. I bought my own truck, too, and I still save a bundle. I don't fine myself. Don't fine anybody, between you and me. People's dogs get out. They're curious and adventurous animals."

"I know all about caring for animals. Ravens are curious and adventurous, too. I've had to chase him down more times than I care to remember. But becoming your own dogcatcher? You're a genius."

"Not so much," he said, looking at his hands. Scurvy Doug was a humble man. And a troubled one.

"I can't wait to talk to you more about your dogs," I said. "But now, I think we have an important non-dog-related question you'd like to focus on?"

"I do," he said, still looking at his hands. Tiny beads of sweat formed on his upper lip. "I think I may have—done something irreversible. But I don't know for sure."

"Hm," I said. "That's interesting, and a new question for me. I thought I'd heard everything. Is there a reason why you don't know if you did anything wrong?"

"I'm embarrassed to admit it," he said, squirming in his chair. "But since I'm taking these measures to figure out what happened, I'm going to be honest with you."

"You can trust me," I said. "Nothing we discuss here will leave this room."

"Okay then," he began. "Sometimes when I drink, I don't remember everything."

"You black out?"

"I do," he said. "I thought blackouts happened to everyone. One or two of the other guys would have a hazy recollection of something they did or said, but not like me."

"You must've been very distressed when you made the realization that your drinking may be different from other people's," I said. "I'm so sorry. How can I help?"

"Let's start with a reading, I guess." He sat up straight, wanting to be a good student. "How do we do it?"

"First, you shuffle," I said, handing him the cards. "Any way you'd like. I think we'll do a five-card spread for you."

"Five-card spread?"

"Yes, it's a good choice for variations on a theme. In this case, the theme would be whether you did the thing you think you did, and any other information you need to be aware of in relation to the question. Does that sound like a plan?"

"It does," he said, visibly shaking.

"Do you want some water?" I wondered if what he needed was a greasy breakfast and some ibuprofen.

"No," he said. "I'm fine. A little nervous."

"If you're done shuffling—take your time, there's no rush—then place a card in these five locations." I pointed out the pattern to him.

He did so.

I flipped over the center card, which is the card that sets the theme for the five-card reading. It's the card around which the others revolve, so it connotes the central issue. "This is the main theme around the central question of whether what you did was irreversible."

It was the Hanged Man.

Scurvy Doug swallowed. "Am I going to hang?" he asked, his eyes shiny, his leg shaking.

"Not at all," I said in my most reassuring voice. "We're not going to take this card literally." I gave him a little smile. "You're in limbo. You don't seem to know or understand what is happening to and around you. This not-knowing makes it diffi-cult to make decisions."

"Sounds right," he said. "I don't—I don't remember."

I could see the tension in his jaw. I flipped over the remaining four cards.

"This card in the upper right-hand corner is the Nine of Swords. I recently pulled this myself in a reading, and you can see I'm still standing."

"She's crying," he said.

"Correct," I said. "This card shows how upset you are. You have so much anxiety you can't sleep. See how she's in bed?"

"I've had trouble sleeping. A lot on my mind."

"Of course," I said. "You're overwhelmed. Something is out of control in your life—and you know it." I knew about his drinking problem, but it wasn't my place to say anything. I only hoped, by acknowledging his suffering in a non-judgmental way, that Scurvy Doug would begin to prioritize his health.

"Look at this one," I said, pointing to the Ten of Swords in the upper right-hand corner. "This looks bad, I know." I laughed a little to try to lighten the mood—Scurvy Doug was openly sweating at this point. This card comes directly after the Nine of Swords. It's the next card in the deck. And although this person appears to be lying on the ground and stabbed with an arsenal of cutlery, I assure you this is better than it looks."

"How so?"

"It's rock bottom," I said. "This is the worst it's going to be. Right now. This burden you're carrying? You want to put it down and carry on with a new life."

He wouldn't look me in the eye.

"Are you ready to move on?"

"I don't know if I can take much more," he said.

I eyed the spread. It wasn't sunshine and rainbows, I'll admit. If I could keep him with me, I could offer a small ray of hope.

"Let's try this one," I said, directing his attention to the lower left-hand corner. "The Five of Pentacles. You feel exiled, alone. Like no one understands you." I didn't want to put too fine a point on it, but I was finding the literal interpretation of this card very interesting, considering the circumstances. "This card can denote job loss or financial ruin."

"This card looks bleak," he said, his voice cracking. "The snow. The crutches."

"Think about what you might be using as a crutch," I said. "Anything resonate?"

"It does," he said. He put his head in his hands.

"Look up, Doug," I said. "I want to show you there's hope. See how they're walking past the stained-glass window? The window is illuminated. Help is available to you. All you need to do is ask."

He seemed to shrink in his seat.

I kept going. "The last card we'll talk about today is this one. The Moon. This is a major arcana card. It's powerful and has a significant impact on your reading."

"Look at the dogs," he said. "I have dogs."

"You mentioned your dogs before," I said, delighted the card was relevant. "This card is not a warning, exactly. It's letting you know you should trust your intuition and be careful moving forward on any decisions. You might be reacting before you have the information you need."

From my perspective, this was an excellent end to a stark reading. I believed he knew he needed help, and if he trusted his intuition, he would get it.

He looked green. He swallowed. I worried he might throw up.

"Doug, I—I know this seems heavy, but this is a better reading than you think it is."

"You don't know me," he said. He finally met my gaze. "You don't know me at all."

I was falling victim to something Aunt Inez had warned me about with readings. I could hear her voice say, *'A little knowledge is a dangerous thing.'* From the way Scurvy Doug was reacting, I had to wonder if we were talking about the same thing. Was this reading about his drinking? Was the moon card telling me there was more going on with Doug than what I saw on the surface?

Scurvy Doug stood up and said he had to go.

"The cards are not necessarily a prediction," I said, trying to salvage what remained of our cordial interaction. "The cards offer insight and awareness. They're stories—they give you another way of looking at your situation or advice on how to move forward. Please, before you do anything rash, take a beat. Maybe spend some time with your dogs and have a big lunch. Then, if you want, you can come back here or call me to talk about it. Doug?"

He was halfway out the door when he called back, "Thanks, Carrie," he said. "You've done enough."

"Doug—" The door slammed behind him.

As he turned to walk up the street, I thought I caught a glimpse of the corner of a brightly colored scarf poking out of the top of his back pocket.

Chapter Twenty-Five

Was one of Baba's scarves in Scurvy Doug's pocket? Why would he have it? And why would he be carrying it around?

I shook it off as a coincidence and cleaned up my space. Stormy came in, bearing coffees and a smile.

"How'd it go with Doug?" she asked, handing me a paper cup.

"My lips are sealed," I said, quietly dying to tell her about the scarf in his pocket. "Can't discuss it. Where have you been?"

"I needed to see Titanic about some legal stuff this morning, no biggie," she said. "He's helping me with a problem, and I think we solved it." She clicked her cup on mine, like she was celebrating some good news.

"What took so long?" The back of my neck prickled, but I was determined not to start a fight before I heard her out.

"I thought it would be a quick touch base," she said. "We got to chatting. And then when I came back, I saw you in here with Doug and I didn't want to interrupt. I got coffee. You're right, though. I'll let you know beforehand next time." She kissed me on the forehead.

"You're in a good mood. Your eyes are all twinkly." Exuberant Stormy was the best version, so I decided to forget whatever was bothering me and join in the fun. We'd been under so much stress. What possible good could come from me whining about whether she left another note?

"I am! I handled a small-yet-sticky issue. Picked up delicious coffees. And now I am about to squire my best girl and her irascible doom chicken to my favorite place on the planet—The Shipwrecks."

"Waggery's coming too?" I was starting to get excited about the idea of an outing with the three of us. I looked forward to shutting my brain off for a little while and letting the sand, sea, and surf inspire me.

"He's going to love it," she said, bounding up the stairs. "Let's get your bird and get you into some warmer clothes. It's blustery out there."

"It's blustery everywhere," I said under my breath. But I was grateful for the offer.

I emerged from Stormy's closet long-pantsed and rubber-booted, with a thick wool beanie, and an overcoat that could easily stand up to gale force winds.

"Aye, aye," I said. "I'll be needin' a pipe to complete my Captain's garb."

"You look like Paddington Bear," Stormy said.

"Fine by me. It's the first time I've been warm since I got here. I don't care if I look like Santa Claus."

"I'm looking for Waggery's leash," Stormy said. "I think we might need it out there."

"Quok," Waggery knew the word 'leash' and was already making a fuss. "No," he said. "Oh, no. No."

"Stormy's right," I said to him. "But we'll wait to put it on. See? It's going in my pocket."

Satisfied, Waggery hopped onto my shoulder.

"You ready?" Stormy dropped the gun into a plastic bag.

"Guns make me edgy."

"It's not loaded. It's in the bag. And it's about to be gone forever."

"That's a good thing," I said. "I feel like I need to talk to Diving Bill. I'm nervous something's going to happen to my ring."

"Like what? It's evidence, right? It's not going anywhere."

"My mood would improve if I could get it back today."

"You don't have the paperwork yet."

"If I can talk to Diving Bill, he'd—"

"Let's deliver the boomstick to its final resting place," Stormy interrupted. "It's dangerous, and I don't like having it any more than you do. We'll swing by the coroner's office when we're done doing the deed if you're still feeling icky."

"We have a stolen ring and a flash drive from a dead woman whose house we broke into. We're throwing an illegal firearm into the sea. Did I mention I saw the gray lady today?"

"What? Where?"

"She was snaking through the streets of Mariner's Cove like she owned the place. She must be from around here."

Stormy appeared to be lost in thought. "Maybe. Or she visits often. Either way, the whole thing is shady. Where exactly did you see her?" She typed something into her phone.

"Slippery Eel lane maybe?"

"*Aargh*," Waggery said.

"Perfect," she said, still typing. "You guys ready to go see some cool stuff?"

Waggery giggled, and I watched as the two of them tussled in a quick play fight. If I could have frozen the moment in time, I would have. Despite all the twists and turns in our relationship, I couldn't imagine sharing Waggery's affection with anyone else.

"We have two options," Stormy said. "Stay here and be shady. Or take care of business."

"I think it's a combo—we're doing shady business."

"So says you." She opened the door and motioned for us to join her. "I think we're two ladies in love going on a walk by the sea. Nothing to see here."

"Nothing to 'sea'?"

"I don't charge extra for puns," she said. "Let's go. I've got a gun burning a hole in my bag."

Chapter Twenty-Six

I was glad to be bundled up when we arrived at the parking area for The Shipwrecks. The wind was powerful and cold, and my jaw juddered with every blast.

"Whoo!" Stormy said, putting on her gloves. "I think you should leash Waggery. Look at those guys."

Sea ravens, a sizable conspiracy, dove and plunged over the bluffs. They spotted Waggery instantly and circled and swooped to get a better look. I didn't get a feeling they would harm him. They seemed curious. But I wasn't sure how he'd react to the attention from a flock of ravens nearly twice his size and much more comfortable in this environment.

He was so distracted by the aerobatics of these graceful flying beasts he hardly noticed when I snapped the leash onto his leg. I was glad. The wind whipped all around us, and I didn't know if I could handle a physical conflict with a stubborn raven.

"It's not as windy where we're going," Stormy said. "You'll feel safer on the beach. C'mon."

"There's no sign. No trailhead," I said, shouting to be heard over the gusts of frigid wind.

"Correct," she said. "Titanic wasn't kidding. People know about The Shipwrecks, but the pirates work hard to keep them out of guidebooks, tourism articles, and online maps."

We hiked along a bluff. The drop was vertiginous, and the waves mercilessly pounded the shore below. Sea ravens looped above, crying out to each other and, presumably, to Waggery, but I had no way of knowing what they were saying. I'm not sure Waggery did, either.

"People would come from all over to see this," I said. It was inconceivable to me that an entire beach was filled with historic ships and no one offered tours. The Shipwrecks could be a magnificent money maker in the right hands.

"They did offer tours, for a while, a few decades ago," Stormy said. "Eventually this beach became attractive to vandals. And a girl drowned. It's slippery and dangerous."

"Oh, no," I said. "Terrible."

"Oh, no," Waggery said.

"She was trapped inside the hull of one of the ships when the tide came in," Stormy said. "Titanic was the attorney representing the family. He convinced the town council to shut down public access and got them to agree to building a coalition of locals to keep most people out. I have a permit." She pulled a rumpled piece of paper from her pocket.

"How do you get one?" I asked.

"You take a special class and get safety instructions. You, madame, are technically out here illegally. But don't worry, I'll make sure you adhere to all laws and regulations."

"I like how you have a permit for a beach, but not for your firearm," I said.

She held her finger up to her lips. "Shhh. Don't tell anyone."

My laughter stopped when I saw The Shipwrecks. The wind died down to a slow, lilting breeze. The air became warmer, the surf quieter. It's not the kind of beach where you'd go dashing into the water to splash around, but it was decidedly less tumultuous than the shoreline I had so far encountered in Mariner's Cove.

But if the serenity of this hidden cove instilled in me a sense of peace, the ruins that loomed above us stole my breath.

Five ships lay on their sides, as if the hand of some playful god had reached down from heaven and dropped them on top of one another like forgotten toys. They were wooden ships. I would've believed Stormy if she told me they were authentic pirate vessels. And despite some weathering, a couple of charred beams from ill-advised beach fires, and a tiny bit of carving from young people in love, they were very much intact.

"What are they? How—"

Waggery flapped and tugged at his leash. To him, they looked like tunnels or caves, and he wanted to explore.

"They look so pirate-y, don't they?" Stormy said.

"Like they belong to Captain Hook," I said. "What are they?"

"Russian fur trader ships," she said.

"Oh, no," Waggery said.

"Not feathers," I said to him. "Fur. Plus, they don't hunt anything for fur around here anymore. Right, Stormy?"

She'd run up to one of the ships and was scrambling into it.

"This is the farthest spot into North America the Russians came for trading and hunting," she said. "No more hunting for pelts these days. Or feathers. Come on up here!"

"Is this okay?" I stood at the base of the ship, watching Stormy clamber up the side like a pro.

"Yes! Be careful not to break anything. Light steps. Don't pull on stuff."

Waggery stayed calm as I gently made my way over the side of what I guessed was the hull of the ship. The way they were all laid on their side, tucked up next to each other, created an obstacle course that Stormy made light work of. I would have had an easier time if I didn't have a four-pound bird on my shoulder, but I loved having Waggery here with me. The Shipwrecks were magnificent.

I ducked under masts and hoisted myself over the sides of ships until I joined Stormy at the fifth one. We stood in an opening of the hull, a hole gnawed open by decades of hungry waves. Sea spray splashed my face. Waggery fluttered up and down, not quite sure what to make of the cold salt water.

"This is the place," Stormy said. She was positioned at the edge of the ship and was about to step onto the boulders that formed the only barrier between us and the ocean water. "When the tide's in, you can't get out this far. I'm going to climb up and chuck the gun in. Come on."

I wanted to join her, but the rocks were equally jagged and slippery. The water was hard-charging and deep and sloshed around the base of the boulders. I didn't want to think of what would happen if I fell in.

"I can't," I said. "My rubber boots don't have much grip."

"Oh, man," Stormy said. "You sure? Light foot it. Like the floor is lava."

"Now you've convinced me I need to stay put. And I don't want to risk it with Waggery. If anything happened to him, I'd never forgive myself."

"Makes sense," Stormy said. "You stay safe. I'm going to do the deed."

"Do it!" I said. "Get rid of your gun!"

She pulled the gun out of the bag and raised high in the air. "Avast, ye, Hearties! Let this terrible curse be gone!"

"Send it to feed the fishes!" I shouted.

Stormy cocked her arm back. As she heaved forward, she slipped. The gun plunked into the water a few feet from her. She struggled to stand.

"Stormy!"

When she stood, she was knee-deep in the wash, and the foamy water swirled all around her, pulling her down and shoving her back into the side of the ship with every wave.

Waggery flapped and screamed. I searched for any safe passage to get closer to her.

"Floor is lava," I thought. I took a light step, landed on the toe of the boot, and wedged it into a crevice. It worked!

"Carrie, stay there." Stormy was out of breath, but she was able to move. "I got this."

As Waggery hopped up and down on my shoulder and shrieked in my ear, Stormy hoisted herself back inside the hull. Wet and cold, but no worse for wear.

I almost cried with relief. With all the secrets, stolen items, and other skullduggery that had plagued me since I'd been in Mariner's Cove, the last thing I needed was to lose Stormy to the sea.

I grabbed her in a tight embrace. "Thank goodness you're okay."

Waggery gave her kisses. "Mwah."

She pulled away and pushed my damp bangs out of my eyes. "I'm okay. I'm here."

Stormy had blown into my life with gale force. We didn't always understand each other, but I knew we had a strong bond. Thinking I could lose her because of some kind of chaos I brought to her life filled me with terror. I knew I loved her. And now I also knew I could no longer imagine my life without her.

Stormy caught her breath and glanced back at the waves crashing one after the other, eternally. "I didn't throw it as far as I wanted. But the backwash, the currents and the undertow are powerful. I'm sure it's a mile offshore by now."

My eyes flooded with tears, but I didn't want her to know how scared I'd been. I wanted to be tough, like her.

"Nice shot," I said, my voice completely devoid of fear, pain, and sadness.

"I aim to please," she said, playing along. She lightly punched my shoulder. Such a Stormy move.

"Quok," Waggery said.

"You've got excellent range," I said.

"Good one." Stormy was already scrambling out of the ship. "Now, let's get you out of here. We're both cold and wet, and we've got some clues to sort through."

Chapter Twenty-Seven

When you have an animal companion as bright and intuitive as a raven—especially one who gets continual care and attention like Waggery—it's easy to believe you know what they're thinking. I always knew when Waggery was hungry, when he needed a walk, and when he wanted to play. I could predict when leaving him home alone would result in a torn-up pillow or an emptied and strewn-about trash bin. And I was so in tune with his needs that, most of the time, I could prepare what he needed before he knew he needed it. Over time, my ability to care for him had become second nature. It was a privilege to provide this intelligent, emotional creature with everything he needed to thrive.

But as we wound our way back to the car from the grandeur of The Shipwrecks, I couldn't read what he was thinking. His mood was melancholic. I sensed what could best be described as *longing* from him, and I wondered if his encounters with these charismatic sea ravens had awakened something primal in him. Did he feel like he was missing out?

"What is it, friend?" I asked, giving him a nuzzle. "Why so blue?"

He returned my affection, which calmed me a bit. "Aaargh," he said, without his usual cheer.

"You wanna be a pirate?"

"What's going on?" Stormy had slowed her pace a bit to walk alongside us. I noticed her lips were turning blue, but I kept the observation to myself.

"I think Waggery's feeling sensitive about the sea ravens," I said. "I don't want to assume, because I don't know, but the ravens in Prosperity are usually dumpster diving or harassing him from the trees. These ravens are wild and big, and full of life. He's smart enough to see the difference."

"Those ravens are pretty cool, Waggery," she said to him, looking right into his eyes. "They don't get to live with the lovely Carrie, though."

"What a nice thing to say." She could be so charming. "I know he loves living with me, with us. He's seeing a whole new way of being a raven. And he's in thrall. Plus, he probably misses his girlfriend." Ligeia was a duck who lived at Prosperity's duck pond. He saw her every day on our daily walks, and he may have been feeling homesick for his routine.

"Can you let him off his leash?"

"Quok," Waggery seemed to agree.

"Absolutely not," I said. "No way. Too dangerous.

"You don't think he'll come back?"

"I'm not sure," I said. "He's good in Prosperity, but he knows where we live, and his flight radius is contained. It's wilder here, and the wind is stronger. Plus, I don't know these ravens. They could be territorial. He could be attacked."

"Seems like a bad idea," she said. "Maybe we can bring him for more walks here. Leashed, of course. He seems to like it."

"Great idea," I said. "I get it. I want to fly away with those sea ravens, too."

Waggery knew we were talking about him, and he fussed and flapped.

"Let's get him home," I said. "We'll come back soon, okay, Wags?"

* * *

When we pulled into town, I checked my phone. I'd lost service near the shore and was curious to see if anyone had called. Was I hoping Diving Bill had had a change of heart? That he'd hand over the ring because he'd seen it in my possession? Maybe. He was a good guy, and he seemed to want to help me. And I wasn't opposed to begging.

"We should swing by," I said. "It's right on the way."

"I don't think we should bother Diving Bill." Stormy sounded annoyed. "You still need to get all the paperwork to prove the ring is yours. We have a file and a flash drive to go through. I think our time is better spent investigating her files. Get everything ready, present him with irrefutable evidence, walk out with the ring. Right?"

"It's right on the way," I said. "What's the big deal? You can stay out here with Waggery, and I'll pop in to see if there's news. I want to be a pest, so he doesn't forget I need to get my property back."

"I think—"

"You think what? Why don't you want me to go in there? You're acting like you're hiding something."

She cracked her neck and bit her lip.

Was she trying to keep herself from saying words she'd regret?

"Fine," she said softly. She maneuvered into a parking space. "You're right. Keep shaking the trees. Waggery and I will wait here for you."

"I'll be quick," I said.

"Here," she said, leaning over and handing me a quarter. "Put this in the meter. The meter maids here can be deadly. You've got fifteen minutes."

* * *

"Nice hat," the lady behind the counter said as I walked into the coroner's office. "Looks like a William Fitzwilliam original."

I laughed. "You're probably right," I said. "My girlfriend loaned it to me. Day at the beach."

She mock-shivered. "It's cold out there! Did you have a good time?"

"We did," I said. "We took my pet raven, Waggery, and he seemed to have a real emotional response to the sea ravens, the way they are so wild and unfettered—what beautiful creatures."

I could see her eyes glazing over. She had no idea what I was saying.

"Never mind," I said. "It was nice. But I'm here to check on my property. Is Diving Bill, I mean, Mr. Fitzwilliam, here?"

"Sorry, dear. He's out. I can have him ring you when he gets back."

I cracked a smile at the pun, but kept my thoughts to myself. "Maybe you can help."

"I'll certainly try."

"This is—delicate," I said. "I don't wish to be disrespectful. But Baba Caracatiță had a ring lodged in her throat and it belonged to me. Has there been any update?"

"Okay, I do not know what all those words you said mean, but I did talk to another young lady about a ring about an hour ago."

"Was it a big emerald?"

"Huge," she said. "Biggest gem I've ever seen. It would look amazing on her."

"What do you mean?" I asked. "The ring belongs to me."

"That's curious," she said. "A young woman came in early this morning and asked about it. Mr. Fitzwilliam stood right here and told her she needed proof. He won't release the ring without the papers."

A fist formed in my guts. "Who was she? Where did she come from?"

"No idea," she said. "I will mention our conversation to Mr. Fitzwilliam. He'll contact you if there's anything more you need to know."

A lump had formed in my throat, and I could barely get my words out. "Please, have him call me, Carrie, as soon as he can. It's my ring."

"Okay, dear," she said. "I will."

I turned to leave and stopped before I opened the door. "What did you mean by 'it will look amazing on her'?"

"Oh, the woman? The ring is an emerald."

"I don't understand," I said.

"Redheads always look beautiful in emeralds," she said. "Don't they?"

Chapter Twenty-Eight

I felt like I'd been kicked in the stomach by a Titanic-size buccaneer's brogan. I was angrier than I'd ever been. And more hopeless.

Stormy took one look at me and said, "You need tea. Stat."

We returned to her loft in record time.

Waggery flew to his perch and groomed himself quietly. It seemed like we were both dealing with emotional fallout.

I paced the room. "Who is this woman?" And what does she want with my ring?"

"I'm making you a sandwich," she said. "You'll feel better when you eat."

I desperately wanted to talk to Grist. Stormy was being supportive and helpful, but Grist had a special understanding of my connection with Aunt Inez and knew how much the heirloom meant to me. Her house was one thing—I was honored she left it to me. But I felt her presence in the ring, and I loved how I could look down at it and know she was with me. I also believed Grist would have information about Baba's ring and its connection to Stormy's and mine. I was sure he'd have a clue to help me unravel some of these secrets. I knew he had information he could share, information to lead me to the cloaked lady.

But he was unreachable. So, what would be the next best thing?

"Stormy, I'm calling LeMarcus Green," I called into the kitchen. "I'll be on the balcony. Privacy and all."

She shot me a thumbs up after she tossed a piece of cheese to Waggery, who caught it in mid-air.

I brought the laptop with me, turned on the gas fire pit, and settled in to go over some documents with a man I'd never met.

He picked up on the first ring.

"LeMarcus Green," he said. "Is this my favorite buyer from Prosperity?"

"Uh, no," I said. "I mean, I don't think so? But if you're talking about Grist, I'm associated with him."

"To whom am I speaking? I saw a number from Prosperity, so I simply assumed."

"My name is Carrie Dettwiler—"

"Carrie!" he said. "THE Carrie? The one Grist raves about?"

"The one and only," I said, relieved I wouldn't have to go into a long and confusing explanation of how I knew LeMarcus.

"I've been meaning to come by and get a reading from you," he said. "I've been seeing this woman, and she's driving me insane—"

"I would be delighted to meet with you any time," I interrupted. "If you can help me with the problem I'm having, I'll give you a lifetime of free readings."

"Sounds more than fair," he said with a laugh. "What can I do for you, Grist's Carrie?"

With nothing to lose, I told him everything.

I mentioned he and I had spoken once before. We'd had a brief phone conversation right before the wine museum burned down during the previous year. At the time, he didn't realize he was speaking to me. I told him about Baba and the mysterious way she died. I told him about the ring and why I needed documentation and how important this was to me.

He was silent for too long after I finally stopped speaking.

"You still there?" I asked. "Did I scare you away?"

"Carrie, this is delicate." I heard him shuffle some papers. He cleared his throat. "You obviously know Baba was my client. She was an interesting woman. Passionate about her collections, and flawless in her ability to sniff out valuable items. I'm going to miss her. It's tragic."

"I'm sorry for your loss, LeMarcus," I said. "She seemed, um, vibrant."

"I need to see you in person," he said. "There's much you don't know. But first, I need to talk with some folks to see what I can tell you."

"I know a little about Ravenous Partners," I said. "The most important thing to me is getting my ring back."

"What about the other two rings?"

My chest tightened. Did LeMarcus know there were other rings, or was he fishing?

I tried to speak, but nothing came out. Could I trust him?

"Carrie? Are you still there?"

"Yes. I'm still here."

"Are you—are you aware there are three total rings?"

I couldn't answer.

"Your silence can mean yes or no," he said. "I'm going to take a swing and guess that you do know there are three. Correct?"

"I have one, Stormy has the other. And the coroner here in Mariner's Cove has the third. I don't care about the other two. I only want the one the coroner has."

"Now we're getting somewhere. What do you know about these rings?"

"Virtually nothing," I said. "I have more questions than answers."

"Unfortunately," he said, hesitantly. "There are several other people who are hunting for these emerald rings."

The hairs on my arms stood up, and not from the chill. "What do you mean?"

"I can't talk now," he said. "The original papers you need are in Baba's house. There are people who may have known, and they may have obtained them already. I'm coming to you tomorrow, and we're going to break in and get all the evidence she has. If we can."

"It's a crime scene," I said. "I don't think we can go barging in there."

"Then we're going to have to be careful," he said. "I'll meet you there at nine."

Chapter Twenty-Nine

Stormy and I had stayed up most of the night, attempting to understand what was happening, who was involved, and why we kept getting swept up into plots of intrigue. We laughed. We cried (mostly from exhaustion). And I marveled over how sharp she was, how she thought of every angle. The contrast in our thought processes was on full display. Once again, I was trying to find ways to work with the people we knew and cared about. She was busy dissecting her interactions with everyone to find the lie, the grift, the misdirection. We'd had very different upbringings.

"How do you know you can trust LeMarcus?" Stormy asked as I got dressed.

"I don't," I said. "I can only assume he's a good guy since Grist has done business with him for so long. He knew about the three rings."

"You sure you don't want me to come?"

"I want you to come, but my gut is telling me two is too many, much less three," I said. "Plus, Waggery needs a sitter. I can't take him with me, and he's not going to like it. We missed our walk this morning."

"It's you and me, buddy," Stormy said, giving Waggery a kiss on his beak. "Hope you like scrambled eggs."

"He'll love you forever if you give him eggs," I said. "No salt, though. Wish me luck."

"I'll call Titanic when you get arrested for breaking and entering," she said.

"I hope you're joking."

"Not joking." She was holding Waggery like a baby and bouncing him up and down. "Have fun! Don't get murdered!"

I'd worried about whether I could trust LeMarcus, but my concerns were about theft or a con job. I didn't think he might kill me.

"You think he might—"

"Of course not," Stormy added, seeing how concerned I looked. "Joking. No one's going to kill you. I don't think."

I gave them both a big hug. "I love you guys."

"Be safe," Stormy whispered. "I mean it."

I flung open the door and skipped down the steps, through the tattoo shop, and onto the sidewalk.

Without Waggery slowing me down, I arrived there faster than before.

LeMarcus stood waiting in Baba's garden.

We introduced ourselves and shared pleasantries. He seemed eager to dive right in.

"You know all about Baba," I said. "Obviously you know about this mysterious part of her house."

"Indeed, I do," LeMarcus said. I noticed he glanced quickly over his shoulder. "Why don't we step inside?"

I followed him in and once again marveled at Baba's collection.

"She wasn't a fortune teller," I said. "Was she?"

"Teresa would dabble," he said. "She was a collector of mystical items. She resold at a profit, and she did the whole

Baba thing as part of the branding. Her alter ego. In real life, she was plain and mild as a bowl of vanilla yogurt."

"Descriptive." I decided against sharing what I already knew and let LeMarcus talk. "Teresa is her real name?"

"Teresa Cascada," he said. "She was Baba Caracatiță."

"How did she come up with the name? What does it mean?"

"Caracatiță means octopus in Romanian," he said. "She liked that it was difficult to pronounce, and had, in her words, 'flourishes.'"

"I don't follow."

"When she read cards, she used an extremely rare tarot deck with pictures of sea life, starfish, crabs, and octopi. It was called the *Regina Tentaculeour*. You may have heard of it."

"Doesn't ring a bell," I lied. My eyes darted to the deck on Baba's reading table.

"It was a name, not much more. Let's get what we came for and I'll fill you in on these details later. We shouldn't get caught in here together."

"Where does she keep her files?"

"Teresa was an organized woman, so no doubt she had electronic copies of everything. Probably on that flash drive you mentioned before. But you need the original document, and you won't find it there. Where would she keep special papers? A safe, perhaps?"

I surveyed the room, which was still as cluttered with memorabilia as it had been on the day Baba disappeared.

I looked under the rug for a trap door. The ceiling didn't seem to have anything unusual about it. LeMarcus seemed equally stumped.

I checked out the bookshelves again, hoping for a clue.

"Maybe we should use this Ouija board," he said, holding

up an elaborately decorated board that looked old and authentic. "Not joking."

"You give the Ouija board a try," I said. "I'm going to check out the literature."

Once again, I was perusing Baba's bookshelf for clues about something I didn't yet fully understand.

If I'd had sticky fingers, I'd have been going home with quite a few of Baba's treasures. The antique tarot cards were, of course, marvelous. And there was a glass Ouija board that would look gorgeous on Aunt Inez's coffee table. She also had a collection of first edition classics worth a fortune.

"Look at this," I said. "All fourteen *Wizard of Oz* books."

"Those are all signed. I helped her find them. Fun project." LeMarcus said, his eyes still trained on the Ouija board. "Move, little guy. Tell us where the papers are."

"It's called a planchette," I said. "I'm fairly certain you're not going to find an answer on the Ouija board."

He stopped suddenly and looked up.

"What is it?" I asked. "Do I need to find a local priest?"

"No," he said. "The Ouija board hasn't possessed me. Is there an Oz book about emeralds? Emerald City?"

"This one?" I pulled out *The Emerald City of Oz* and opened it.

An envelope rested inside.

I replaced the book, sat down at the table with LeMarcus, and opened it.

He grinned from ear to ear as I unfolded the papers.

"It's a map," I said. "A map?"

"It is," he said. "It's all the proof you need to show anyone who doubts your ring belongs to you."

§

I'd finished one of my first solo readings and was briefing Aunt Inez on how it had gone. Not particularly well.

"I tried to explain to her, but she wouldn't hear it," I said, throat tight, eyes filling with tears. "All she wanted was a definitive yes or no. When I told her we were writing a story, she said all she cared about was the last page."

"How did you leave things? Was she upset when she left?"

"She refused to pay. Said she hadn't got what she wanted, which was a decision about whether she should leave her husband for cheating. I told her what the cards said and explained the nuances. But she demanded. I said, 'I'm only seventeen. How should I know about your marriage?' She stormed out."

Waggery, listening from his perch, snickered. I think Aunt Inez attempted to suppress a smile, but that was also her resting face, so it was hard to tell.

"You did the right thing," she said.

"She didn't pay!" I cried. "She's upset with me. It's not right."

"Correct. It's not right she demanded you predict the future. Not because of your age, but because tarot is a narrative. A reading is far more likely to reveal what your client is already thinking and feeling than to reveal the mystic future." She waggled her fingers in a woo-woo kind of way.

"How can I explain that to people? She didn't get it."

"It sounds like you need a different example." She took her deck out, shuffled a few times, and laid out a Celtic cross, ten-card spread. "I always thought the closest metaphor for tarot was writing a story. But perhaps, if we look with fresh eyes, we can see it's a map."

"A map?"

"It's not a perfect metaphor," she said. "Follow along anyway. We place a card in the center, and then we work our *way to the cards around it, revealing new information and insights as we go. We never change the order; we follow the map. We read the signs. We draw conclusions, but never make predictions. You don't use a map to predict the outcome when you arrive at your destination. You use the map to see how you're going to get there."*

I gazed at the spread before us and tried to wrap my head around this new way of thinking.

"You're not going to take a detour in your reading, right? It's leading you to a destination—the final card of the spread. Then you put it all together, read it, and determine your steps. It's factual. Like a map."

"The cards are like road signs?"

She considered my simile. "Yes. They're road signs. We don't argue with road signs. We exit when we're supposed to. We turn on the correct street. In life and in tarot, Carrie, stick to the map. Always stick to the map. The map leads us to treasure."

§

Chapter Thirty

I'd seen provenance papers quite a few times in my life because my Uncle Grist had single-handedly built a wine museum in Prosperity. But the papers in my hand didn't look at all like the ones I'd seen Uncle Grist carrying around.

"Where's the bar code? Where's the prism sticker with the serial number? The signatures? The official stamp?"

"Good eye," LeMarcus said. "If your tarot thing doesn't work out, I'll bring you on board."

I was oddly flattered.

"The map and the rings are linked," he continued. "One doesn't work without the other. Do you understand?"

"I—do not."

Footsteps.

Upstairs.

Voices.

"We need to get out of here," he mouthed to me, and I agreed.

We tiptoed out and closed the door quietly behind us.

"Is your car up there?" I whispered.

"No way," he whispered back. "It's in town. I came up the

path."

"Aren't you curious about who's in there?" I for sure wanted to see.

"No, ma'am. Let's go."

We hotfooted it down the hill into town.

"I don't think anyone clocked us," he said. "Not sure, though."

"Me neither." I looked around. "Town's pretty quiet today, all things considered."

"Is there a place we can go?" LeMarcus asked. "We can look over this. I'll try to explain what I know."

I thought for a second. Stormy's wasn't an option because she was there with Waggery. The Shipwrecks were private, but the weather out there was hardly conducive to a low-voiced conversation.

There was only one other place I knew.

Barnacle Brandon gave a nod as we ducked into Down the Hatch. I indicated silently we were going to a booth in the back corner, and he gave a thumbs up.

"I've always wanted to come in here."

"Food's great," I said. "Get the seafood stew."

I was relieved our server wasn't someone I knew. Not a pirate. A normal guy. We ordered our food, and then I spread the map out on the table in front of us.

"Please," I said. "Explain to me how this map—as cool as it is—proves anything belongs to me."

He put his hands on the table in front of him.

"Where'd you go right now?" I asked.

"Sorry," he said. "Collecting my thoughts. We have a lot of history to cover, and I want to be sure I don't leave anything out. Now, I need you to understand I don't know everything, and I haven't met all the players. But I have been involved in some, how should I put it? Transactions. Over the years."

"The best place to start is at the beginning," I said.

"Okay." He took a deep breath and began. "Your Aunt Inez was a remarkable woman."

"I know." Hearing her name reminded me of how much I missed her.

According to LeMarcus, my Aunt Inez, a venerable, respected citizen of Prosperity, joined forces with a group of forward-thinking residents to boost the profile of our town. Founded by Agustus Hoggarty, who made his fortune and then built a remarkable vineyard and winery estate in the heart of Prosperity, the town had an interesting history, but it had always been overshadowed by other winemaking towns in the region.

"Ravenous Partners, they called themselves. A nod to your aunt's pet bird. Name was Wiggly."

"Waggery," I corrected. "He lives with me now."

"He's still alive?"

"In captivity, ravens can live up to eighty years. Waggery's probably around forty."

"Fascinating," he said. "Does he still talk?"

"He does." I was getting impatient. Yes, pet ravens were a fascinating topic, one I could usually go on and on about, but I didn't want LeMarcus to lose focus. "If you finish your story, I'll take you to see him."

LeMarcus looked starry-eyed. People often got excited about Waggery, and more than a dozen people had offered to buy him from me.

"Oh, gosh," he said. "I'd love to see him. I would. Fond memories."

I had to stop myself from snapping to get him back on track.

He recovered his composure and continued.

Aunt Inez's boyfriend, the man I refer to as Uncle Grist, was instrumental in getting projects off the ground. He formed the Prosperity Historical Society and began raising funds for the wine museum—the very one I nearly died in when Flynt Burns torched it. According to LeMarcus, Grist and Inez believed unique, informative attractions could siphon off some of the tourist business from Napa and Sonoma. They were also behind the development of the duck pond in the center of the town plaza.

"You have no idea how controversial the duck pond once was," I said.

"Oh, I absolutely do," he said. "There was enormous push-back, even from the Partners. They wanted less free stuff and more high-end boutiques, like Michelin-starred restaurants. Then the schism began. There were those who believed Prosperity would be better served by a few public attractions everyone, including the locals, could enjoy. And then there were those who wanted Prosperity to be a luxury destination. They were perfectly willing to force out the long-term residents to cater to people who'd pay top dollar for perfect weather and frou-frou restaurants."

"Inez and Grist were the ones who wanted things to be local-friendly," I said. "Farmers' markets and festivals as opposed to swanky boutiques and spa hotels."

"Exactly. They were being edged out, so they left before things got ugly. And you know what happened after. Mayor, dead. Emma Fort-Knightly, dead. Flynt Burns in big trouble."

"I nearly died, too," I said. A bitter bile rose in my throat. All of this death over what? Money. Again.

"This information lines up with what I already knew," I said. "But what does any of this have to do with the map?"

"Here's where things get murky," he said. "I'll tell you everything I know, but there are questions you'll need to find the answers to."

"Fire away," I said, confident nothing could surprise me anymore.

Boy, was I wrong.

According to LeMarcus, Grist and Inez were stung by the attitudes of their fellow Ravenous Partners and agreed to step back. As a show of goodwill, the now-deceased Mayor Preston Brix allowed Grist to complete his work on the wine museum.

"My job," he continued, "was to assist Grist in procuring unique specialty items for the museum. And then we found out the originals were being returned for full refunds and replaced with fakes."

I was getting antsy. He was repeating facts I already knew. Facts that led to Flynt Burns trying to burn me alive. This wasn't a conversation I wanted to have. I was ready to move forward.

LeMarcus sensed my frustration. "We'll put a pin in it." He shifted in his seat. He took a sip of his Earl Grey and slurped some stew.

"I was working on a small side project for Inez. About her ring."

I perked up. This is the information I wanted to know.

"Did Grist know?" I asked.

"If he didn't at the beginning, he did later. But he's probably missing key details. We all are missing key details."

LeMarcus explained how my aunt showed him an emerald ring and explained it was one of three.

Three rings. Three initial recipients. Three rings scattered to the wind over time, upheavals, and chaos.

"You tracked down the ring, and then what?" I asked. Was LeMarcus more wrapped up in the ring mystery than I had thought? My head told me I could trust him, but my skin crawled at the prospect of inviting yet another person into my drama.

"I did. We have sleuthing in common," he said. "Inez was very adamant about needing the map, not only the rings."

"Okay..." I said, trying to suss out clues. "If she had the rings, why did she need the map? Isn't the map telling you where to find the rings?"

"Not at all," he said with a mischievous smile. He dabbed his lips and put the napkin back in his lap. He was winding up for a big reveal.

"The map tells you where to find the treasure. The treasure Inez wanted *you* to have."

What treasure? I was suddenly much more interested in this map.

"I have a ring," I said. "Stormy has a ring. Baba had a ring. How does Baba fit into any of this? And if my Aunt Inez was adamant about the map, why wasn't it in her fireplace with my ring? Why did Baba have it all the way up here in a town I don't even live in? Why isn't my name on it? Or Stormy's?"

"I wish I could tell you. I wasn't privy to every discussion and transaction. But you're going to be blown away when I tell you the next bit. And you'd better be glad I'm an honest sort because if anyone else knew about this ..." He paused. "You could be in danger. It's a treasure, after all."

His tone concerned me. Was he thinking what I was thinking? He had to know if he gathered the rings with the map, then he'd have access to this purported treasure. Was I in danger from LeMarcus?

My curiosity overrode my desire to bolt, break into the coroner's office for my ring, grab Stormy and Waggery, and go into hiding. "Tell me. I want to know everything."

"The rings must be together. Without all three, you can't access the treasure. I don't know how they work, or where they go, or what to do with them once you've gotten there. But I strongly believe you need the power of all three to make a claim."

I sat back in the booth, totally overwhelmed by what I was hearing.

"You think others might know about this?"

I watched as he figured out the best way to word this next part."Carrie, they probably do."

The statement was jarring, but true.

"Study this map," he said. "I'm sure there are clues."

"I'm still confused. There's nothing on this map that makes it clear that my ring belongs to me. How can I use this to convince the people in charge that they should hand it over?"

The bill arrived, and I reached to pick it up. LeMarcus grabbed it before I could.

"I got this," he said. "When you find that treasure, I expect you to treat me to dinner in one of Prosperity's finest establishments."

"Will do," I said. "Hope you like High on the Hoggarty, my friend Hank's place. The fourth-best burgers in Prosperity, six years in a row."

He laughed. "It'll do, it'll do."

We sat together amicably. I gazed at the map.

"This artwork is stunning. I wonder who made it."

"Here's a key," he said, pointing to a small box in the lower left corner. "These symbols could mean anything. I see a lot of this in my line of work. It's part of the fun."

This was no straightforward map. It was crawling with symbols and Latin phrases in addition to the landmarks. I didn't think we'd be able to look at this and figure it out without solving its mysteries. I needed Stormy. She was good at puzzles.

"Sorry," I began. "I still don't understand how this proves to Diving Bill or anyone else that I own the ring that was given to me."

"Pass it over here, and I'll show you."

I did so. He eyeballed the map, turned it upside down, and flipped it over. "I'm looking for the matching maker's marks."

"Maker's marks?"

"Your ring, and the other two, bear these marks. Ah, here they are, hidden in the compass rose. See? Right there?"

I leaned in. The center of the compass rose bore a circular drawing of three ravens, each with an emerald-green eye. Their wings were open, and they grasped a golden ring with their talons. One wore a small hat, like the Pied Piper's. One wore a tunic with a corkscrew shape. And the third was emblazoned with an evil eye.

"Did you ever notice one of these shapes on your ring?" LeMarcus asked. "These symbols are the maker's mark. Your ring will have one of these images engraved on the inside."

I sat back in my seat. "Mine's the evil eye. I haven't looked or seen it, but I bet dollars to donuts that the evil eye one is mine."

"Why do you say that?"

"Inez's nickname. Evil I. Get it?"

"Well, how about that?" He smiled.

"I bring this map to Diving Bill and say my ring has an evil eye on it and it matches a map. How does that get me my ring back?"

"I've already thought of that." He pulled an envelope out of his jacket. "In this envelope is the original invoice that I provided your aunt. I've also included a letter, signed and stamped using my credentials, and notarized. It explains the maker's mark and how it connects to this symbol on the map. The map proves ownership and is inseparable from the rings. When the map and rings were created, there were no barcodes or serial numbers. I think having the map along with my letter should be sufficient to prove to the bureaucracy the ring is yours. If they still drag their feet, we can go to court."

I had no interest in court, but I was so grateful to LeMarcus I didn't want to say anything negative. "Thank you, LeMarcus. You've thought of everything."

"I'm excited to see what you do with the information," he said. "Looking forward to the phone call telling me you've found a fortune."

A figure on the map caught my eye.

"Beryl Bay?" I asked. The room went wobbly. "Here, in the upper corner of Lake Liminal?"

"It might be," he said. "The paper is so old. Might need a strong light and a magnifying glass. Does Beryl Bay have meaning for you?"

I debated whether to tell him. We were having such a nice time.

But it slipped out before I knew what I was saying.

"I do know a few things about Beryl Bay," I said. "I know it's in the High Sierras."

"Ah, Bigfoot country," LeMarcus said. "I had a Sasquatch experience up there myself—"

I interrupted. As much as I wanted to hear about LeMarcus's cryptid encounter, I'd been hit in the sternum with a cannonball. "I know it was a significant hub during the California Gold Rush, and it's rumored there are untapped veins and hidden fortunes in those hills." The words were coming out of my mouth as if I had no control over what I was saying, as if I'd been possessed.

"Yes," LeMarcus said, interested. "A reasonable place to expect a treasure."

"There's one other teeny detail about Beryl Bay on the north edge of Lake Liminal in High Sierra Sasquatch country."

"Yes?" I could tell LeMarcus loved trivia, so what I was about to do pained me.

"My parents died at Beryl Bay."

Chapter Thirty-One

After the awkwardness of my bombshell passed, and we ran out of things to say, I made good on my promise to take LeMarcus to see Waggery.

Waggery immediately flew to LeMarcus's shoulder and showered him with kisses.

"Mwah," Waggery said. "Mwah. Mwah."

"Would you look at that?" LeMarcus said, clearly charmed. "What an astonishing creature. Thank you so much for letting me see him again."

"You're welcome," I said. "He seems to love you. Come by anytime you need beak-kisses."

LeMarcus laughed.

I held out my arm, and Waggery flapped over to me.

"You've got a lot to sort out, Carrie," LeMarcus said. "Call me if you have any issues with this guy at the coroner's office. Or anything else."

"Your number's in my phone."

"Good luck," he said, opening the door to leave. "I sincerely hope you find your treasure."

"Makes two of us."

In the quiet of Stormy's apartment, a few things became apparent to me. If what LeMarcus was saying was true, Aunt Inez may have set me up for a life where I no longer had to worry about money.

This was dangerous territory for me, emotionally.

I never let myself think I would be rescued from my debt. I always believed I would work my way out of it somehow. My basic needs had always been met, Waggery was well maintained, and I had people in my life who cared enough about me to keep me off the streets. I recognized this as a privilege, and I refused to feel sorry for myself.

Mostly.

What might it be like, though, to unearth a treasure that could release me from financial insecurity? What indulgences might I treat myself to? First, I'd pay off my student loans, of course. And any back taxes. And everything I owed to my friends. Then, I'd build Waggery a play structure in the garden filled with toys and enrichment activities. Then what? I'd buy a new cell phone.

Could I even dare to dream I might be able to afford a practical, used, mid-range sedan with excellent mileage?

I got goosebumps thinking about it.

I shook off the fantasy. There was no time for daydreams. I wanted to tell Stormy everything first and then I was going to spin on over to Diving Bill's office, present him this map with a flourish, and get my ring back.

That's when I realized Stormy had agreed to babysit Waggery while I was out.

Where was she?

Why had she left him alone?

I checked my phone. No text. There was no note on the kitchen counter or coffee table.

What could have been so important that she would abandon Waggery? How long had he been alone?

Stormy had crossed a line. My nausea turned to fury.

I closed my eyes and tried to calm down. I heard Aunt Inez's voice in my head, '*When you don't know what to do, do the next right thing.*'

The next right thing was to ensure Waggery wasn't injured. He fussed at me when I checked out under his wings. I searched the floor for feathers, peered into his eyes (clear, bright), and peeked under his tail.

"You look healthy," I said, giving him a peck on the head.

"Quok," he said, forgiving me for the violations. He fluffed his feathers and started to purr.

"Next right thing, next right thing..." I repeated the mantra, hoping to conjure it from mid-air.

"When in doubt, pull a card out."

I picked up my tarot deck from Stormy's coffee table and tapped the cards a few times to wake everybody up.

A few shuffles later, I made a stack. I held the deck in my hands and thought about my question.

"What's the next right thing?"

I pulled a card.

Ace of Pentacles.

A single hand reached out of a storm cloud to present a large gold coin. Underneath this giant, sun-sized doubloon was a rose arbor, under which a path led to a mountain range. Lilies dotted the way, ensuring peace for the journey.

The Ace of Pentacles was a positive card in a reading, but what did it mean here, for me, right now?

"This is a card of action," I told Waggery. "Of seizing the money, the clue, the opportunity. I'm on the right track by thinking I need to move."

I quieted my mind and focused on the image. What was it telling me?

It's telling me to go get my ring.

I'd wanted support from Stormy, to run my plans past her before showing up at Diving Bill's with a map and a wild story about treasure.

But Stormy wasn't here, was she?

"Let's be bold," I told Waggery as I put on my denim jacket. He flew to my shoulder and sat, rather than stood, giving me a warm feeling, like he sensed my distress and was comforting me.

Then he nibbled my earlobe.

"Okay, enough," I said. I snatched the map off the coffee table and tucked it inside my jacket. I grabbed Waggery's leash.

"Let's go get what's ours."

Chapter Thirty-Two

"You can't bring animals in here," the lady behind the counter at the coroner's office said in a voice much squeaker than I remembered.

"We'll only be a minute," I said. "Plus, look how cute he is."

Waggery, on cue, blinked his eyes, fluffed his feathers, and purred.

She sat back down, mollified. "Make it quick. Is he a bat?"

"Bat? No. He's a raven." I said, shocked someone from Mariner's Cove might think Waggery was a bat. Whatever, I needed her on my side. "I need to speak with Mr. Fitzwilliam. Quickly, please."

She buzzed me into the back, and I hustled down the hallway to Diving Bill's office and knocked.

"Carrie!" he said. "You were on my mind. Look."

He held up a stretch of the knitted green scarf that wasn't quite long enough yet, but nicely made.

"My scarf is coming along," I said. "What talent you have."

"Thank you. My work requires lots of waiting, so knitting is what I do. And it's a good way to make friends." He smiled at me.

Waggery hopped off my shoulder and waddled around the floor.

"How nice of you to bring Winery," Diving Bill said. "Up close, his feathers are so shiny."

"Okay for *Waggery* to walk around a bit?" I didn't see much for him to make trouble with in here. A few file cabinets. A wall clock.

"Fine, fine," Diving Bill said. "I enjoy him."

"We won't be long. I have proof of provenance."

"You do?" he said, leaning over his desk. "Terrific. I hope it wasn't too much trouble for you."

"None at all," I lied. I didn't need him to see me sweat. "It's my ring, so of course I had access to the documents."

"Of course you did," Diving Bill said. "I'm delighted for you. And I'm sorry you had to endure suspicion and prying. It can't have been easy for you."

Waggery fluttered to the top of a bank of file cabinets behind Diving Bill, and was poking around in a small, potted philodendron.

"Nothing's been easy for a while," I said. "I'd like my ring now, please." I held out my hand.

"Indeed," he said. "Give me the papers, I'll make a few copies, and you'll be on your way."

"Copies?" I asked. "Is it possible for me to show you the document and we don't make copies?"

Waggery started tapping on the pot the plant was in.

"Not now, buddy," I said. I motioned for him to fly to me, but he ignored me.

I felt my face flush.

Tap, tap.

"We need the copies for the file," Diving Bill said. "Otherwise, if someone else makes a claim, how will I be able to prove I gave it to the right person? Someone else showed interest, as you know."

Now, I was angry. "You don't own it, Bill. You don't own this ring and yet you're telling me I can't have what is my property unless I let you make copies of the papers. We both know it's mine."

Tap, tap, tap.

"I understand why this feels... invasive to you. It's been a difficult time. Here's the thing, Carrie. I have the authority to keep this ring forever. The ring can go into an evidence locker somewhere and no one, not even me, will know where it is. I like to follow rules. My job is to follow rules. And what I'm asking is standard procedure."

I looked at the floor.

Tap, tap, tap, tap.

"I get it," I said, knowing I needed to get hold of myself. "This experience has been triggering for me. I'm sorry. Here," I began to take the map out of my pocket.

I heard scraping sounds.

Then, the unmistakable clamor of a ceramic pot breaking into pieces on the tile floor.

"Dammit, Waggery," I spat, unable to control the anger in my voice. "I'll clean this up, and of course, I'll replace it."

Diving Bill stood up quickly. "It's no bother. I'll take care of it. Get the papers ready and I'll make copies when I return." He left.

"Waggery," I pleaded. "Not now."

"Now," he said, in my voice.

He disappeared underneath Diving Bill's desk. I heard scrabbling.

The sound of something small and metal falling to the floor.

Waggery had destroyed the lock on Diving Bill's desk drawer.

My whole body itched, like I was about to break out in hives. No way was Waggery's behavior okay. We were both going to end up in prison.

"Come out right this second, Waggery," I said. "This is serious."

He emerged, like a phoenix, from underneath the desk and posed on Diving Bill's mouse pad. He spread his wings to their full span of nearly three feet, pulled an item out of the drawer, dropped it, and crowed like a rooster.

My ring.

In a split second, Waggery picked up the ring and swooped out of the room.

"Waggery!" I called, giving chase down the short hallway. "No!"

The door buzzed. Diving Bill opened it. Waggery shot through, with me close behind.

"Sorry!" I called. "Something came up!"

"Carrie! Come back here!"

Diving Bill's voice faded as I chased Waggery through Mariner's Cove's twisty alleys. He flew at eye level and right out of reach of my outstretched arms. I tried to call out to him, but I was too winded.

He swooped and twirled. At one point, he rested atop a drainage spout on a stone church styled to look like a gargoyle.

The visual of Waggery posing proudly, as if he owned the town, was dramatic and awe-inspiring. I wasn't angry anymore; I was frightened. For him. For the ring. I couldn't see it from my vantage point, and I was terrified he'd dropped it.

"Waggery, wait right there."

He was in the air by the time I finished the sentence. I caught a glimpse of the ring secure in his beak and relaxed enough to not have a panic attack in the street.

I followed Waggery to Think Ink.

The tattoo shop was closed; all the lights were off. We ascended the stairs to the apartment, and I'd never been gladder to be anywhere.

He watched as I climbed the stairs, and when he was satisfied I was done climbing, he dropped the ring at my feet. I scooped it up and put it on my finger.

Waggery stabbed at the lock with his beak.

"Easy, easy," I said. "I have a key."

I let us in. Stormy still wasn't home.

Chapter Thirty-Three

I'd lived alone for three years before I met Stormy, with nothing but my grief and my raven to keep me company. So many days I'd been low and lonely, longing for someone to share things with—the news of the day, a joke, a snack.

But I'd been fine. My life, although it wasn't perfect, had worked. I had clients. Waggery. Uncle Grist. Small-town gossips. I enjoyed sunny strolls at Prosperity's duck pond.

My nausea, the vague headache, the sweaty palms—none of this was homesickness. My stress was something else entirely. I was questioning everything in my life.

What's the point of being in a relationship if your S.O. isn't even home when you need to tell them about the literal, actual treasure map you found? A treasure she's probably entitled to at least a third of?

What's the point if she and the mysterious redhead are plotting to steal it from me?

Is that what was happening?

Was everything I was going through a setup?

Had it been a setup from the get-go?

I wanted to run. Head home. Take my things and go.

But I couldn't. If I ran now, what would everyone think?

They'd think I was a murderer. They'd know I was a thief. No doubt Diving Bill would tell everyone what had happened. He might even send the police after me.

He would definitely send the police after me.

I paced the room.

I picked up my cards.

I put down my cards.

I chewed my thumbnail.

I thought of calling Titanic, but what could he do?

Finally, I kneeled down, head in hands, and listened to myself breathe.

I sat there for I-don't-know-how-long when there was a knock at the door.

My stomach twisted.

It had to be the police. You can't swipe things from government offices and not expect the hammer to drop.

I didn't know what to do. Would I lose my ring entirely? My freedom?

Waggery flew to the door and pecked at it.

"Waggery, no," I stage-whispered. "We don't know who it is."

"Carrie, open up. It's Titanic."

Waggery looked at me as if to say, "Well? Aren't you going to open it?"

I did.

"Titanic, I'm glad you're here."

"I've got news, Carrie."

"I do too," I said. "You go first."

"I need you and Stormy to come with me."

"I'd love for both of us to join you, but sadly, she isn't here."

"She isn't?" He stuck his head through the door to see for himself. "Where'd she go?"

"I wish I knew," I said. "Unless it's important, I'm going to pass."

"I need both you and Stormy. Right now."

Titanic looked like he might cry.

Waggery made a sound like a police siren.

"Waggery, *perch*."

He flew to his perch, much to my surprise.

"I can't—" Titanic was in an enervated state. But I'd already had a powerfully unsettling day, and all I wanted to do was figure out my next move.

"You have no choice. I might need a statement from each of you."

"I don't underst—"

"It's Scurvy Doug," Titanic said quickly. "He turned himself in for the murder of Baba Caracatiță."

Chapter Thirty-Four

I couldn't believe what I was hearing. Of course, I'd go help, whether Stormy came along or not.

I grabbed my phone, wrapped myself in the warmest jacket I could find, and walked to the door.

"Be a big boy, Waggery," I said. "I'll be back soon. I'll follow you, Titanic."

I left Waggery with a silent prayer he'd stay out of the trash, drawers, and closets, and accompanied Titanic to the police station. We hurried down the street, me taking four steps to each of Titanic's two, and I could see the stress on his face. My heart ached for him. He was a big man with a big heart. I could see why the pirates admired him so much.

We arrived at the station, where a scrum of townsfolk had gathered to get a peek at the confessed murderer. Titanic and I nudged our way through the crowd, though in reality it was more like the seas parted to let him through, and I tagged along like a nervous mascot. He spoke in serious tones to a man behind a counter and disappeared into a doorway.

I waited and checked my phone for updates from Stormy. Nothing.

I smiled awkwardly at one of the gawkers.

Titanic returned.

"I'm officially Doug's attorney," he said. "I'll speak with him now, but they won't let you in."

"Right. Okay," I said, feeling more useless than ever. "I'll go back to the loft? Wait for you there?"

"Doug's beside himself. Inconsolable."

"Poor Doug," I said. He seemed so fragile. Very un-murderery."

"Carrie, there's something you should know. It's why I came out to tell you in person rather than sending you a text."

He looked nervous, which made me nervous in return.

"I'm all ears," I said. "What is it?"

"Doug told me he turned himself in when Office Maigret told him you're suspect number one."

"Oh, no," I said, noticing how weird it was that Waggery didn't repeat my words since he wasn't there.

"I'm going to get to the bottom of this," he said. "You can help."

"Anything." I perked up. I wanted nothing more than to keep busy. And knowing the police thought I might be a suspect made me want to get out of there.

"You know his dogs?"

"I don't," I said. "He mentioned them in our reading the other day. If I was in his same position, I'd be worried about Waggery."

"He'd feel a lot better if he knew someone looked in on them," Titanic said. "They need to be fed and tucked inside for the night. He lives around the corner on Pufferfish Lane. You can't miss it. You'll see the pups out front. They're good dogs, but there are a lot of them. Call me if you have questions while you're there."

I wrapped my jacket tight around me, ready to brave the cold outdoors.

"Before you go," Titanic said, "did he say anything I need to know when you read his cards?"

"My readings are confidential," I said. "If I remember anything I think could help him, I'll share. See what he says, and you and I will talk tonight. I can decide then if I'm holding onto information that could help his case."

I arrived at Scurvy Doug's house quickly; I'd been lost in thought on my way, wondering where Stormy was, feeling sorrow for Doug and Baba. I barely remembered making the turn out of town and down the lane. I almost forgot the cold. Almost.

I could hear the dogs before I saw them, and when I arrived, they barked more, excited to see a person. Doug had a large, fenced-in yard, and the dogs—I counted twelve of them—had plenty of room to romp and play. He'd set up a few agility tasks for them, and there were toys and balls strewn about. His dogs appeared healthy, bright eyed, and vigorous, and, if I'm being honest, I wasn't quite expecting that.

Poor Scurvy Doug, I thought. I bet everyone underestimated him.

But why did he kill Baba?

Did he kill Baba?

Or did he only think he killed Baba?

I didn't know enough about anyone involved to make a case one way or the other, but my senses were tingling. Something wasn't right.

The dogs yipped and yapped and jumped over one another. A one-eyed beagle. A few lab mixes of various ages and maladies (one was missing an ear; another an entire leg), a handful of pitties, and one or two border collies.

These weren't chihuahuas and pugs, so when I unlocked the

gate, pulled it toward me, and stepped into the yard, I didn't have a chance.

I was felled by a lab mix with huge paws. He lunged at me and knocked me backwards into the dirt. The breath left my body on impact with the ground and confusion took over.

It was a canine stampede; every single dog was out of the gate and running as fast as it could toward the coast.

My hands were scraped, I was covered in mud, and my spinal column felt like it had been pounded with a sledgehammer. Stunned, I sat there without a thought in my head.

Aunt Inez would have said I had the wind knocked out of me, and I'm sure this is what had happened to me. Out of fuel. Out of ideas. Out of my mind.

Thinking of my aunt was a wake-up call. I had to save the dogs.

I stood up and looked around to see if there were any stragglers I could easily corral.

Nope.

They were all gone.

Didn't they know I was here to help?

Doug's Animal Control truck was parked in the driveway. Surely the keys were in it?

Time moved like molasses.

I wasn't cut out for this level of stress.

As I wiped my muddy hands on the front of my thrift store dress, I succumbed to a longing for the bright sun and happy flowers of Prosperity. Everything in Mariner's Cove was gray, sad, dirty, and wet.

The baying of a beagle snapped me out of it.

Hallelujah! The keys were in the truck. I climbed in, revved the engine, and headed west.

My first catch was a spotty gal with a sweet smile, who seemed to understand this was part of the fun. I pulled over and flung open the back of the truck, which had one long door that swung out to reveal two dog-sized compartments. I unlatched the wire door on one of them.

She jumped in with nothing more than a weak whistle from me.

I closed the crate. She sat and thumped her tail, grinning like she'd won a game.

"Good," I said, calming down a bit. "Clearly, we've done this before. They know how to get in. Now let's go round up the rest."

After a few minutes piloting the truck around, I found the beagle and one of the pitties, a squat guy the color of pencil lead. Both sides of the truck had compartments. I opened one, and one of the border collies leaped in, curled up into a donut shape, and let out a deep sigh like she was tuckered.

"Easy peasy," I said. "Eight more. I think?"

I drove to where the road ended and found myself in a makeshift parking lot at a scenic overlook.

Eight dogs ran straight toward town when they saw me approach.

I'd done my fair share of chasing down animals, what with Waggery being a bit—ahem, stubborn—about coming home. But all these? All at once?

I was officially flummoxed.

I checked my phone for updates. Nothing from Titanic. Nothing from Stormy.

The surf washed over everything below. It was treacherous and gorgeous. A troop of pelicans floated by, serene and oblivious to my struggle.

This flash of beauty made me think maybe Mariner's Cove wasn't so bad.

I decided I would decide about Mariner's Cove later.

Right now, I was four dogs down, with eight to go. Or was it five down, eight to go? I couldn't remember.

"Must be the Mariner's Cove curse," I said. "Everyone has multiple jobs. Guess I'm the dog catcher now."

I allowed myself to be amused by the thought on the bouncy drive into town, conveniently forgetting it was my fault the dogs were running around Mariner's Cove unattended.

My tiny smile quickly transformed into a frown when I parked the truck in the center of town and got out. Dogs, dogs, dogs everywhere.

Dogs were jumping on people, knocking trash cans over, and running in and out of shops.

"This town's gone to the dogs," I heard someone say.

I didn't have time to roll my eyes. A dog that looked like an unholy mix of corgi and wolfhound was flinging oranges from a fruit stand into the street while the hapless owner looked on. Two others were fighting over a takeout container they'd dragged out of a trashcan. And one guy—a Weimaraner?—was running down the middle of Mainsail Street, howling.

"Don't panic, Dettwiler," I said to myself, surveying the scene. An orange bounced off my foot. I picked it up and returned it to the fruit seller.

"You're the dogcatcher?"

"Only temporary. The regular guy is in jail for murder."

"Huh?"

"It's a whole thing," I said, turning my attention back to the canine-led chaos as it unfolded around me.

Judging by the shocked look on her face, she could have used an explanation, but I had no time.

I thought about calling Titanic, but I didn't want to trouble him, especially since this news would be terribly distressing for Scurvy Doug.

I had to focus. And I had to figure out how to round up these dogs and get them home safely.

I opened all the side doors except the occupied ones, revealing eight additional crates for the dogs. I hoped there'd be a few more who'd jump in, and there were. They came running as soon as they heard the rusty squeak of the hinges.

I closed them in, fetched a handful of leashes off the front seat, and set off to collect the rest.

I'd learned something from Waggery. If you chase an animal, especially a smart one, they treat it like a game. They'll run farther, and I wasn't willing to risk it.

Ignoring the dogs completely, or at least pretending to, I slowly walked to where the downtown business area gave way to a wider road, a small picnic area, and a parking lot.

Then I took my time walking back, jingling the leashes as I went.

No eye contact, Dettwiler. Keep on walkin'.

I heard the tippy-tapping sound of toenails on pavement. I had one!

Mindfully, calmly, I led the dog toward the truck.

Without turning around, I said "Up," and gestured to an empty crate. She jumped right in, cute little gal.

Now I only had to rinse and repeat.

For what seemed like hours, the residents and tourists of Mariner's Cove watched me walk slowly through the street, gathering dogs like some kind of lethargic pied piper. When I closed the final one into the cab of the truck, the people who'd gathered broke into applause.

I took a slight bow and started to cry.

This was all so Carrie. Trying to help but making a mess of things.

I scooped up as many still-rolling oranges I could find and returned them to the owner of the fruit stand, who thanked me.

Then, with help from strangers who were complimenting me, I cleaned up all the trash.

One nice lady, who smelled like freshly baked cookies and reminded me so much of Aunt Inez, put her hand on my arm.

"Don't cry, dear," she said. "Life is messy. But look at us, we're all chipping in to help you clean up."

"Thank you," I said, wiping my nose on my sleeve. "This day hasn't gone as planned."

"Nothing ever does," she said, and somehow, she disappeared into the fog.

"Show's over!" someone called out, and the crowd dispersed.

But before I could get into the truck, I spotted one more orange on the edge of town.

I jogged over and picked it up.

When I turned around, I found Stormy.

Finally, I thought.

She was in a dark stand of eucalyptus, her back to me, embracing a redhead in a gray cloak.

Chapter Thirty-Five

The dogs howled in the truck.

Despite being numb with shock, I had a decision to make: let Stormy know I'd caught her mid-embrace with a gray ghost or focus on the task at hand.

Do the next right thing.

Easy. In this case, the next right thing was to fix what I'd broken. I would return the dogs to their home, where they would be safe, and feed them. I could sort out Stormy later, after the animals were properly secured.

The truck joggled along without a peep from the pups. I drove slowly and carefully, avoiding sharp turns and most of the bigger potholes. I wouldn't have been able to live with myself if any of the pooches got injured back there.

I pulled into Doug's driveway and stopped in front of the gate, which I'd left open. One by one, I led each dog into the pen on a leash, and shut the gate behind me, making sure no one was able to scoot past.

A grueling twenty minutes passed until I'd shuttled them all inside the fence, looking happy and tired. I climbed into their enclosure, and with a pack of yipping dogs nipping my ankles and otherwise trying to get my attention, I figured out where the food was, fed them, filled their water dishes, and made sure they had everything for a safe night at home.

My clothes were filthy, and I smelled like dog, but I'd accomplished ... something.

Before I attended to the various messes in the truck, I counted fourteen dogs.

Fourteen?

I thought there'd only been twelve.

Oh, well, I thought. I couldn't be responsible for every stray dog in Mariner's Cove, and at least the extras were safely penned up.

"Nice work."

My heart nearly shot out of my mouth. A tall man in green coveralls stood in Scurvy Doug's driveway.

"Seaweed McGee, right?" I said after I realized I wasn't being mugged.

"Yes, ma'am," he said. "You're Carrie. Good of you to come down here to help. I came over because I knew Doug'd be losing his mind about his dogs. He loves those puppers."

"We had a little adventure," I said. "They're all okay, but it's been a wild afternoon."

"I heard. The whole town heard. But looks like you got it under control. 'Cept you got Mrs. Yee's chiweenie in there, and I believe that fella is Spike's Jack Russell."

"Oh, boy," I said.

"Don't you worry," he said. "I'll return the wayward ones and stay here to care for the rest. No way Scurvy Doug did what he thinks he did. Doesn't have it in him. Baba could've snapped him in two."

"I know," I said. "I feel awful he turned himself in to protect me."

"I know about his confession, too," he said, looking me dead in the eye. "You're about to be too busy to help with these dogs. I don't know if you did it or not, but I'm willing to give you the benefit of the doubt. You and Titanic are gonna have your work cut out for you."

"Stranger in a strange land sort of thing?" My mood sank even further.

"All's I know is this," he began. "No one's been murdered in Mariner's Cove in the thirty years I've lived here. Now we've got a woman dead, and the only thing changed here is you."

The dogs continued to yap, and the sound was making my temples throb. I could only assume if Seaweed was talking this way directly to my face, the entire town must be on fire with gossip about me. Gossip was the grease in the gears of every small town.

"Do you think I did this, Seaweed?" I steeled myself for his response.

"Dunno," he said. "Maybe we should read the cards."

I didn't like the look in his eye. I didn't like the edge in his tone.

It was my cue to leave.

"Thanks for your *kelp* with this, Seaweed. And for the heads-up. *Sea* you around."

I didn't linger long enough to see if he appreciated my puns.

The gray skies were drawing darker and grayer. I had a few options. I could go hang around the police station to see if Titanic needed anything. I could go back to Stormy's.

I could run.

Snatch Waggery, grab my things, and disappear.

I'd caused more trouble than I'd solved in Mariner's Cove. Stormy was clearly occupied with the ghost, and I wasn't ready to face the reality of what her hidden relationship meant for me. I'd been betrayed. Moving forward with her seemed impossible. Grist had Lillian now, so I didn't feel as comfortable troubling him with the comings and goings of my life. Plus, they were still abroad.

There was no one for me to turn to, and I had Waggery to worry about, of course. If I went to prison, what would happen to him?

I wondered if selling the cottage in Prosperity was the answer. I could easily live off the proceeds if I decamped to a hidden town in Mexico.

The thought was overwhelming.

I stopped and took a breath. What was the next right thing?

The only answer was to go to Stormy's and face whatever awaited me there.

I wanted to put all the lies and secrets on the table and decide what was best for us.

Or what was best for me.

I walked slowly through town as the fog rolled in, and I arrived at Stormy's on the edge of the night. I fed Waggery, played fetch with him for a while, and realized how late it was. I'd heard nothing from Titanic—not a huge surprise, but also not comforting.

I didn't have the heart to peruse the map or sort through clues.

I waited and waited until I fell asleep alone on the couch.

Stormy didn't come home.

Chapter Thirty-Six

My decision became easier as the hours ticked by with no message from Stormy.

Should I tell anyone I was leaving, or did I simply vanish into thin air?

Every bone in my body was crying out to leave town, to get on the road back to Prosperity, and to return to the warm companionship of Uncle Grist and my sunny backyard garden. But sometimes what your body needs to do and what your emotions want to do are at cross purposes. Before I drove anywhere, I needed to pull myself together.

I needed to wrangle Waggery into his crate for the ride home. Crating was a tough sell for Waggery when he was well rested, well fed, and on a routine. Cramming him in there without one of us getting our feelings hurt was going to be a challenge. Not only would he feel uncomfortable for the next two hours, but it was also highly likely he would get carsick. But I had no choice. He couldn't be loose in the car for anything longer than a quick trip. Forty miles was too much.

I made swift work of packing up. No need to employ my usual over-organization to this task. I found everything I owned, shoved it all into my bag, and was done after a few trips up and down the stairs. After I secured his crate in the back seat, I fetched Waggery from his perch in the loft and ferried him down to the car.

With an abundance of misplaced optimism, I opened the door to his crate and said, "Why don't you go ahead and hop on in there, buddy?" I hoped my lighthearted, singsong-y tone would mask my anxiety, but this clever corvid wasn't buying it.

"Grrrr," he said, the growl a warning I usually respected. I could count on one hand the number of times in our years together he'd growled at me, and the few times he had, he was warning me of impending danger. I had no choice but to ignore him because I'd made up my mind; we were skipping town.

"I know you're mad, kiddo," I said. "I hope you'll forgive me. But it's time to go home, and you aren't safe in the car unless you're in your crate."

His body vibrated with another deep, low growl, much more menacing than the previous one. Would he bite? I handled him as gently as I could while still making it clear I meant business—and I wasn't afraid of getting sliced by his beak. No matter how each one of us felt about it, he was going into the crate.

Waggery disagreed. He growled again and then let loose a shriek I'd taught him one Halloween. He sounded exactly like a woman screaming—the same trick had gotten me in big trouble before, when Miriam Cringe used it as evidence to promote her theory of how I murdered the mayor of Prosperity. I scanned the area to see if anyone noticed. No one.

"It's okay, Waggery," I said in a reassuring tone. "We'll be home—"

Waggery's scream was the last thing I heard before hitting the pavement.

I awoke from a blackout. My head and neck pulsed with

pain. My vision was blurred. My hearing was distorted, as if everything was being translated through a tin can.

"I finally knitted you a scarf, Carrie."

As I became aware of what had happened, my first thought was that Diving Bill had looped a scarf around my head and yanked me to the ground. My second thought: I'd let Waggery go, and I couldn't see where he was through the (exceptionally soft, was this cashmere?) green yarn.

Both thoughts flung me into a panicked frenzy. I could hear my own heart pumping. For the first time in this freezing cold town, I was burning from the inside out.

I had no time to ruminate on my emotional state or the location of my darling Waggery, though, because Diving Bill yanked me to my feet as quickly as he'd snatched me down.

The scarf was wrapped around my neck like a leash. Diving Bill stood close behind me, holding it tight while he breathed on my neck, controlling me like a puppet. I scanned the sky for Waggery as secretly as I could. If Diving Bill had a reason to attack me with a homemade winter accessory, I couldn't be sure he wouldn't try to injure Waggery.

I didn't see Waggery, and my eyes welled with tears. I was more worried about him out here in this unforgiving chill, this violent wind, in the territory of mysterious sea ravens than I was myself—and I was being kidnapped.

Diving Bill tugged the scarf, hard. "Get in the car."

I stood stock-still, refusal my only power. Surely Diving Bill, the town coroner and knitter of practical fashion essentials, would back down when faced with a formidable foe.

I was dead wrong. He kicked me, hard, square in the back, and I was on the ground on my hands and knees. Before I could react, I was somehow on my feet again. He was using the scarf to control my every move.

Stunned into speechlessness, I did as I was told. I climbed

into the driver's seat; he climbed into the back, still holding the two ends of the scarf together. I was tethered.

"I'm—I'm not sure I can drive like this," I said, telling the truth. Cooperating. My good manners, drilled into me by my Aunt Inez, were at the forefront of this chilling interaction.

Something cold and pointy jabbed my throat. A knitting needle.

"Start the car, Carrie," he said. "We're going to The Shipwrecks."

A sinking feeling in my gut told me this was not going to end well.

I did as I was told, piloting Uncle Grist's car through the narrow streets of Mariner's Cove until we were on the highway heading toward the beaches.

The drive was awkward, painful, and terrifying. I had so many questions, but I'd been struck mute. Why was my friend attacking me? Why was everyone in my life turning on me? Where was Stormy?

Would I ever see Waggery again?

Any other day, a day I wasn't nursing a broken heart, I would've been able to center myself enough to strategize an escape. As it was, my mind was racing from question to question, my eyes frantically, irrationally searching the skies for my raven.

I piloted the car down the hidden, unpaved road toward the shipwrecks. The car jostled and bounced over the holes and bumps, Diving Bill's knitting needle poking me intermittently.

"Here?" I croaked, my voice failing me. "Is this where you want me to park?"

"She speaks," he said. "It's funny, tarot reader. You didn't ask any questions about why this is happening. Did you predict this was going to be the day you were going to die?"

"Do you want me to stop here or not?" I asked. My rage

surprised me. I'd been so full of terror I hadn't noticed how furious I was.

And boy, I was pissed. Who did this guy think he was, grabbing me with a thoughtful gift and dragging me out here to murder me? I had a raven to raise! I had student loans to pay!

"Yes, Carrie," he said, a little too smugly for my liking. "This will do splendidly."

"Perfect," I snapped. I put the car in park, rested both of my hands on the wheel, and waited for his instructions.

"This is going to be easier than I thought," he said. "Don't you even want to know why we're here?"

Interesting, I thought. He wants to brag.

On the rare occasion I got lost or confused during tarot readings, I'd let my clients start talking. Hearing their worries and fears helped me refocus. Perhaps a tidbit about their past would snap me back to attention. If I let Diving Bill talk, I'd have time to formulate an escape plan. I needed to let go of my rage—which had me feeling flustered—and focus on my safety.

"I do," I said, calmly. "Why are you doing this to me?"

"Great question!" he said. "Why don't we go for a little walk, and I'll explain everything."

He twisted the scarf to maintain his hold on me as he opened the back car door and climbed out. "Now, open your door and follow me."

I did as told, and he deftly managed to keep me on my leash from the outside of the car. He wrapped my wrists in matching green yarn that seemed to be as strong as it was soft. He slipped my ring off my finger and put it in his pocket. Getting kicked in the back was better than losing my ring to him.

But the ring wouldn't matter to me if I was dead.

Focus, Carrie.

"It's not following if you're dragging me," I said. I had a whiff of understanding what Waggery must feel on leash days.

The thought of Waggery was a stab to my heart. With a knitting needle. *If I die today, what will happen to him?*

I banished the thought from my mind. I was going to get back to him today. I just didn't know how yet.

"I remember the night we met. You said if you told me your real profession, you'd have to kill me," I said. "Are you about to tell me about your career choices?"

He let out a hearty laugh. "Good one, card reader," he said. "My boss didn't mention how smart you are."

"You've been talking to whoever it is who runs the coroner's department about me?"

I was playing dumb, and we both knew it. A tricky game. But I'd only started to sort out who was who in this mystery. Diving Bill was obviously a bad guy, but he was only the tip of the iceberg. From his talk of a boss, I'd surmised he was the hired gun (so to speak).

"You wish," he said, yanking me along. "Prepare to have your mind blown."

Was Ravenous Partners behind Baba's murder? And, if so, which members specifically? How did Diving Bill fit in with them?

I couldn't allow myself to think Uncle Grist or Aunt Inez had anything to do with these events. They'd gotten out before all of this, right?

Right?

The wind was whipping all around us, and I had to shout for him to hear what I was saying. Being dragged through this bluster—freezing despite the inconceivably plush scarf around my neck—while trying to maintain my composure was a painful struggle. I shivered in the stabbing cold; my knees knocked from fear as we high stepped through the sand toward The Shipwrecks.

We'd somehow managed to make it to the first ship without

tripping into each other, and he shoved me through an opening in the hull.

I was relieved to be out of the wind so I could hear myself think.

"Keep moving," he said, giving the scarf a confident yank.

I was going as fast as I could. We had to clamber up and over, testing our agility, and we both stumbled frequently. My wrists were tied. I skinned my hands, my knees.

When we finally made it into the center of the wreckage, Diving Bill told me to move toward the bow.

"Toward the ocean?" I asked.

The front of the ship yawned toward the Pacific, its bow having been destroyed years before by the weather, rocks, and vandals.

"You know it is," he said. "What we're doing is a modified plank-walking."

"You're going to push me into the sea?" I stumbled clumsily over the wreckage, rocks, and whatever else littered the inside of this ship.

The waves crashed and boomed all around the front of the wrecks, but the tide was still low.

"I'm not doing anything," he said. "Gonna make it hard for you to get out of here, though, and the tide should take care of the rest. It's my specialty. Making it look like an accident."

"Making what look like an accident?" I asked.

I couldn't take my eyes off the water. The tide may have been low, but there was no doubt I'd be dead quick as you could say 'quok' if he pushed me in.

"Your death," he said. "I'm going to be the last person to see you alive, but no one will ever know. Stand there. Back against the foremast."

"Back against the—"

"Do it," he said.

I leaned against the only thing he could possibly be talking about. He pulled the ball of yarn out of his back pocket.

"We're going to wait patiently for the tide to come in," he said. "When it does, you'll drown, this Ladakhi cashmere yarn will wash away along with your body, and no one will have any idea you're even missing until you've been digested by a great white."

I couldn't let him tie me up.

I looked around to see if there was a sharp or blunt object I could use as a weapon. Diving Bill had let his guard down; I had to act.

I wiggled the ring I'd found at Baba's out of my front pocket. "You're going to be wanting this," I said.

He stopped what he was doing. "Do you—do you have the third ring?"

"Maybe," I said, tossing it back and forth between my tied hands, making a show of being clumsy with it.

"Let's not do anything foolish," he said.

I shrugged. "Why is it so important to you?"

He seemed to be stunned speechless. "You don't—," he began. "You don't know?"

I fiddled with the ring. "Know what?"

"You can't be serious," he said, seeming to forget he was supposed to be tying me up. "The Ravenous Rings?"

"Like Ravenous Partners?"

"Yes!" He started jumping around like he'd won a prize. "Exactly! The rings are a clue to a treasure."

I couldn't let him know what I already knew. I only had one goal: survive.

"Then you'd be mad if I—" I gestured toward throwing the ring into the ocean.

"No, no—!" Diving Bill lunged toward me. "You don't know what you'd be losing."

I raised my tied arms in front of me, holding the ring tight in my fist. I edged my way toward the surf. "Would it be bad if I dropped this right now?" I dangled the ring over the water.

"You wouldn't," he said, his hands out in front of him in the universal gesture for *calm down, lady, and step away from the bow of the ship.*

I glanced at the rocks below. I couldn't let on how scared I was.

A flash of light caught my eye.

A spark of silver.

Stormy's gun.

I knew it wasn't loaded. Had never been loaded. But Diving Bill didn't know anything.

The gun was on the rocks. Within reach, if I stretched.

Stormy should've done a better job of throwing her gun. What if it fell into the wrong hands? We were going to talk about this later, which meant I needed to stay alive at all costs.

I turned to face Diving Bill.

"You don't think so? Treasure won't do me any good if I'm dead. Why would I want my murderer to have it?"

I raised my arms and threw the ring as hard as I could over the top of the ship into the sand dunes that loomed above us on the other side. It sailed through the air, out of the ship, and out of sight.

"What? No!" Diving Bill scrambled toward the back of the ship as fast as he could, given the wide variety of sharp obstacles.

No time to worry about the ring. I lay down on my stomach and reached toward the gun. It was at the tip of my fingers. I waggled them to try to reach it and managed to scoot the handle toward me enough to get a grip.

I had it. I was holding a gun.

Game on.

I got up as quickly as I could.

I tripped and stumbled over the splintery wreckage. I dropped the gun a few times and each time I dove to retrieve it, I ended up banging myself up more.

Until I remembered the floor was lava.

"Light feet, tippy toes," I said to myself as I maneuvered much more easily through the ruins. "Small hops. Concentrate. Balls of the feet. Grace of a dancer."

I was lighter on my feet than ever before, confidence gleaned from a ten-year-old boy named Spike.

This was a game, a fun kids' game. Thinking of lava helped me get out safely and swiftly.

"Thank you, Spike," I said when my feet finally touched the sand. "Free readings for life if I get out of here alive."

When I emerged, Diving Bill was scouring the beach for a glimpse of the precious ring.

"How could you?" he shouted before he saw I was armed.

"I'm going to need you to take a seat," I said, wondering if this should be my new catch phrase.

"Where'd you get a gun?" he asked, sitting, his eyes wide.

"I'll be the one asking questions." I took a few steps closer, gun raised, so I could hear him better in the wind.

"Tell me everything," I said. "Now."

"I will not," Diving Bill crossed his arms like a petulant child.

I pulled the hammer, and it made an unmistakable clicking sound.

"I can see you're going to be unreasonable," he said. "If I tell you everything, you want to go in on it? Fifty-fifty split?"

"Fifty-fifty of what?" I had zero plans to go into business with this guy, but I needed him to tell me everything he knew.

"You'd get half of one of the greatest fortunes ever hidden," he said. "Look, I'm your regular, run-of-the-mill assassin-slash-coroner. I specialize in strange deaths. I've never used a firearm in my line of work. Attracts too much attention."

"You were hired to kill me?" I asked. "For my ring?"

"I was hired to get the rings, all three, using whatever tools I had at my disposal. Do with the information what you will."

"You killed Baba," I said.

"Hold on a minute," he said. "Not true. What happened to Baba was an accident. A happy accident, as it turns out, for me. But not intentional."

"Explain," I said, wiggling the gun in his direction like I meant business.

"I saw her slip the ring off your finger during your argument at Think Ink. You were too drunk to notice. I ducked out and went to her house to wait for her. All I wanted was for her to hand it over, along with the one she'd already procured. She swallowed it instead, which enraged me."

"I don't—"

"Then she started to choke on it. There was nothing for me to do but leave. I knew the ring would be safe and sound lodged in her trachea, and I would be called back as an order of business the next day or the day after."

"What about Scurvy Doug?" I said. "How did you get him to confess?"

His eyes lit up. "He's a gem," he said. "He'd threatened Baba in front of a room full of people, and he planned to make good on it. Unfortunately, the old scalawag passed out drunk on Baba's porch before he could get to her. After she croaked, I snatched one of Baba's scarves and stuck it in his pocket as I stepped over him."

I began to see how the events and the players were tied together like a tarot spread in front of me, but I was still murky on the details. "Then Stormy's ring would be the only one left to retrieve," I said. "Was Stormy next on your list?"

"She was the easiest, so I saved her for last," he said. "I was going to disappear her during our next round of Assassin. Simple kidnapping and toss into the ocean. Like today."

"This makes no sense," I said, puzzling it out. "Why keep me alive this long if someone was paying you to kill me?"

"Isn't it obvious?" he asked, leaning back into the sand, like he had all day. "I needed the paperwork. The map. Without the ring, the map isn't worth the paper it's printed on. Without the map, the rings are nothing more than a pile of old jewelry. They belong together. Inseparable."

"You weren't sure who would end up with the map when you got here," I said. "Now we can all die, and you'll have the map, all the rings, and access to a mysterious treasure."

"Do you know how hard it is to kill one person, let alone three? My employer has waited a long time and was in no hurry and was determined I handle things correctly to keep their own hands squeaky clean."

"You let Scurvy Doug take the rap for Baba."

Diving Bill laughed. "Not part of the original plan, but he made it so easy. What a rube. Maybe he'll sober up in there."

"You're cruel," I said. "All this for what? Gold?"

"What else is there?" he asked. "You say 'gold' like it's unimportant. This treasure is unlike anything you've ever seen."

I thought about the other things a person could want. Love with a trusted partner. An animal companion who fills your heart with joy. Family to lift you up.

But then again, I'd had terrible money struggles, and a trunk full of gold wouldn't be a bad thing.

Did he say it was a trunk full of gold, or did I assume?

I looked up to ask, and Bill was standing in front of me.

I held the gun up. I could see it shaking and hoped he didn't notice.

"Why don't you hand over the gun?" he asked calmly. "If you were going to shoot me, you'd have done it by now."

He'd called my bluff, and he could see it in my eyes. I wasn't cut out for criming.

He put his hand on the gun and pulled it out of my hands.

He lifted it in front of my face.

I went completely numb.

He pulled the trigger.

Click.

I knew the gun wasn't loaded. But staring down a firearm at point-blank range had unlocked a new level of terror. He was willing to do anything to prevail.

Diving Bill, weekend pirate and knitter of scarves, had just tried to kill me at The Shipwrecks.

I sank to the ground.

Diving Bill knew he had me, and even without the gun, he could snuff me out in a jiffy.

"Bill," I began. "I'll help you look for the ring."

"No need," he said, walking toward me.

I stood up and stumbled back toward The Shipwrecks.

The sand pelted me, the wind sliced through me. My mind was free of thoughts, as if the panic had shut it off. "*Nothing to see here,*" my brain told me, a protective mechanism. My life didn't flash before my eyes, or even provide a reel of memories, or last-minute regrets. Instead, I experienced a silent acceptance of my fate; a calm understanding that everything was about to end. A curious peace shrouded me in what I believed to be my last moments alive.

"Quok!"

My mind snapped awake. Waggery!

I didn't dare look up and tip Diving Bill off to Waggery circling overhead.

My heart pounded louder than the surf. My beloved friend

was here. Feelings of love and a powerful desire to survive washed over me like a tsunami. I became a force of life, a machine. I'd do anything to stay alive.

I kept backing away from Diving Bill, hoping Waggery wouldn't do anything to try to save me. Not yet. *Stay up there, buddy*, I thought.

I refused to be murdered in front of my bird.

Not today, anyway.

Native ravens had gathered, as if summoned by Waggery. They circled overhead and were making a racket.

Do not look up, I repeated silently to myself. Ravens looped in and out of my line of sight, and Waggery was among them—somewhere. I listened for his distinctive calls, but their sounds jumbled together. I couldn't tell if Waggery was silent, if his calls were being drowned out, or if he had already learned how to mimic his wild friends.

Diving Bill was closing in. "You don't have to do this," I said, a weak attempt at changing the subject.

"What do your cards say?" His grimace alarmed me. Did he think this was funny?

'*The best defense against the Devil is to laugh in his face,*' Aunt Inez told me once. I remembered my recent readings had repeatedly showed the Devil reversed. Here we were, Diving Bill and myself, metaphorically chained together because of this curse, this treasure, whatever it was. And Waggery was flying above, his wings stretched exactly like the Devil on the tarot card.

Could my reading be this literal? Did the Devil card mean I would be in a life-sized replica of the images it depicted?

Then I had a strange recollection. The Devil on the card had bird feet.

Enough. It was time to enlist Waggery's help if I was going to get out of this alive.

"Waggery!" I called. "Waggery! I'm in here!"

Diving Bill could barely contain his glee. "Are you—are you calling for your *bird*?"

He clearly underestimated the horror of being attacked by a four-pound bird with razor-sharp talons and a beak made for pulling gristle off bone.

It didn't matter how I answered, because suddenly Waggery was on him. His talons scraped at his cheeks while he pecked at Diving Bill's head and screeched. Diving Bill cried out and waved his arms about. He struck Waggery a few times, and Waggery took off toward the rest of the ravens circling the sky above the cliffs.

"March," Diving Bill's eyes were wild with fury.

I took a step backward and fell to the ground. Nothing about this was graceful, but he was going to have to work hard if he wanted me to die. I wasn't going to make it easy for him.

"Fine," he said. "I'll drag you if I have to."

Waggery must've thought I'd been injured. He yelled, "Oh, No!"

Diving Bill looked up, no doubt preparing for Waggery's attack. It was my last chance. I kicked him in the groin and scrambled on my hands and knees to where the sand met the cliffs. He doubled over and said some very insulting things.

Waggery stayed in the sky, and Diving Bill advanced again toward me. I had visions of him lugging me by my hair through The Shipwrecks, my body getting bruised and battered before he dumped me into the ocean.

The dune sand was soft. I struggled to get my footing. The gun wasn't loaded. I could run away, I thought, if I could make my legs move through it.

But I couldn't. I kept stumbling.

Diving Bill lunged toward me, grabbed me, and pulled me toward the surf. I screamed in horror, calling him every name I could think of. I fought hard, but I was only exhausting myself.

A sea shanty carried on the wind. I heard the pirates before I saw them scurrying down the cliffs. Most were dressed in their regalia, while others still were in their work clothes (nice Dockers, Seaweed McGee!).

I nodded toward the horde. Diving Bill turned to see what was coming for him.

He raised the gun. The army came to a halt.

"Oh, no!" Waggery called from above.

"He's bluffing," I shouted to the pirates. "The gun's not loaded."

I hadn't seen Stormy mixed in with the group, but as soon as I spoke, she raced out of the pack at full speed and dove toward Diving Bill.

He turned to run, and I scooped up a handful of sand and threw it in his eyes. Stormy grabbed the gun, ran to the edge of the water, and threw it as far as she could.

Titanic rushed forward next, snatched Diving Bill up by the neck of his immaculately knitted sweater, and dragged him off the beach. The pirates jeered, booed, and spit at Diving Bill, turning the spectacle into a grotesque parade as they followed Titanic out.

Waggery dove to the beach and landed on my arm. He pulled the yarn off my wrists.

"Mwah," he said, covering me with kisses.

I held him close and tucked him into my jacket. I kissed the top of his head. "I was so scared I'd lost you," I told him. We warmed each other, and he began to purr.

"I would like to not see your gun again," I said to Stormy.

She was out of breath and had a feral look in her eyes.

"Carrie," she said. "I was so scared we wouldn't make it in time."

"How—?"

"Waggery," she said. "He found me and made such a fuss trying to drag me in this direction I knew you were in trouble. I fetched Titanic, he rallied the troops, and we all came running."

"It was a sight, seeing you all tearing down the hill," I said and watched Titanic effortlessly manhandle Diving Bill up the last of the path.

And as satisfying as it was to know my would-be-murderer was in custody, I realized how close I'd come to death. My heart raced; I gasped for air.

"I think you're having a panic attack, Carrie," Stormy said. "It's okay. You're going to be okay."

The sobs were deep and cleansing. "He wanted to kill me, Stormy," I said, over and over again. Stormy held me tight until I cried out the last of my anxiety.

Waggery had wriggled out from under my jacket and was hopping around on the beach.

I didn't like Waggery being so far away. I called him over. I didn't ever want to be away from him again.

He landed in front of me, his black feathers iridescent in the light, and dropped the ring I'd thrown into the sand. Then he perched on my shoulder.

"Mwah."

"I love you, too," I said. I rubbed his head and savored the slick feel of his feathers. Relief washed over me.

Stormy picked up the ring. "Never gets old," she said. "He's a miracle."

I took a cleansing breath. I shook my shoulders.

There was much to be done.

"Now we have all three," I said. "After we make sure Scurvy Doug is freed, we need to talk."

"You bet, boss," she said, sensing she was in trouble.

The three of us slowly made it up the path toward the

parking area. My legs were weak, but my resolve was strong. I needed rest. I needed a day on the couch cuddling with Waggery. But the day's drama wasn't over.

"Thank you all," I said to the pirates who were milling about the parking area. "From the bottom of my heart. You saved my life."

I walked through their ranks, hugging them, shaking hands. They told me of their plans to follow up with Titanic, offered us more help, and suggested dinner reservations at Down the Hatch. Normal pirate stuff on a normal pirate day.

My heart surged with love for my new friends, my adopted hometown. A rag-tag team of pirates had risked their own lives for mine and Waggery's. And Stormy... She came through for me like she always does. Every time I think I've been abandoned, she finds me, picks me up, gets me to safety. I was alive. And I wasn't going to take my life, my friendships, or my future for granted. There was so much more living I had to do.

I still had questions about Stormy's behavior, but I decided to let the drama die down before dissecting her movements over the last few days.

"You ready to go?" Stormy asked, her hand on my arm.

"I am," I said. "Thank you, Stormy." I wrapped my arms around her.

"Oh, wow," she said. "No need to thank me, ever. I'll always come for you."

I believed her.

We allowed the moment to linger, to ground us, to remember why we were together. She pulled away and wiped a tear from her eye. "Please stop almost getting killed," she said. "I can't take it."

"*You* can't take it?" We laughed a little and pulled ourselves together.

"Next steps," I began. "I need to call Uncle Grist and Lillian. We need reinforcements."

"They'll know what to do," Stormy said. "It seems like the mystery of Baba Caracatiță has been solved?"

"Unfortunately," I said. "This revelation has given me more questions than answers."

Chapter Thirty-Seven

I was still too shaken to drive. Stormy took the wheel to shuttle Waggery and me back to the loft.

"Crank up the heat," I said. I was no longer running for my life, and the cold hit me like a wall. "I'll never get used to this place."

Stormy's face fell as she turned the heat on full blast. "Carrie, I—"

"No," I said. I knew she was about to confess something I wasn't ready to hear. I was settling into the safety of our connection in the aftermath of a terrifying encounter, and I needed to stay in this mental safe space. "No. I don't want to hear any of this yet. We owe it to Scurvy Doug to get him out."

"If I could—"

"I said no. The deaths, arrests, jewel thievery, and shady behavior are bigger than our relationship. Both of our lives are in danger. Once I'm sure we're both going to survive, then you can confess or reveal or share, or whatever. But right now, the topic of *us* is off limits. Diving Bill was going to kill you next. During Assassin."

We drove silently the rest of the way home, Stormy's

knuckles white as she gripped the steering wheel. When we arrived, I carried Waggery inside, put him on his perch, filled his water dish, and put a handful of shelled peanuts in his food bowl.

Stormy and I didn't do silence. Usually, one of us was chatting away about this, that, or the other. But I didn't know what to say to her. I didn't have a plan for how to move forward.

I paced around. Stormy busied herself making tea.

What did one do with oneself after nearly being murdered by a hired assassin? Aunt Inez hadn't covered attempted murder in our tarot sessions.

Should I pull a card?

The answer to this is always yes.

I ducked into the bedroom for privacy. I didn't want to have to explain anything to Stormy.

I shuffled a few times, grateful my hands had thawed out.

Then I plucked a card from the deck and laid it down on the bed in front of me.

Queen of Pentacles.

A woman on a throne, surrounded by abundant beauty, gazing at a gold coin.

Money.

It's always money.

I pushed my bitter thoughts aside. Typically, the Queen of Pentacles is a delightful omen in a reading. She represents the ideal combination of success and virtue. A calm, nurturing spirit, the Queen of Pentacles either confirms you've achieved what you've worked for, or it asks you to seek out this queen in your life for guidance, support, and wisdom.

Since I was nowhere near achieving anything I'd set out to do, I believed this card was asking me to rely on the counsel of someone in my life who has these traits.

Stormy? Not a chance.

Was this Baba? Was she a warm, nurturing soul whose life was tragically cut short? How would I ask her?

The only other woman in my life right now was Lillian, and she and Uncle Grist were gallivanting about Europe right now, probably knee-deep in historic castles, cemeteries, and battlefields.

I needed Aunt Inez, more than ever. I was heartsick for her.

But I wasn't willing to let Stormy see me upset.

With nothing else to be done, I checked on Waggery.

Stormy sat on the sofa, drinking her tea. She'd made a cup for me.

"Have some tea," she said. "Relax."

"Relax?" I began checking under Waggery's wings, his beak, his feet. I didn't see any nicks or scratches, and he was placid on his perch. "Diving Bill kidnapped me, tried to murder me, and I waved a gun around like I was some kind of movie cowboy. I thought I'd lost Waggery forever. I don't know if I'll ever relax again."

She stood up as if she was going to come toward me.

"No," I said. "No."

She sat down without a fuss. "I'm calling Titanic right now," she said, pulling out her phone. "Let's find out what's happening so we can determine the next steps."

"Queen of Pentacles," I muttered.

"What?"

"Nothing, Stormy. Go ahead and call."

According to Titanic, he'd wrangled Diving Bill to the police station where he was being held until Officer Maigret returned. Maigret was apparently working a thorny missing-person case and would deal with this later.

Scurvy Doug was still in custody and would stay there until further notice.

"Why?" I asked. "Shouldn't he be released immediately?" My neck itched.

"Titanic says they can't release him until they have enough evidence to convict Diving Bill," Stormy explained. "He confessed, remember?"

I shivered. "I remember."

Titanic promised to drop by as soon as he could. Officer Maigret would need to speak with me, and he wanted me to be prepared.

"He said it can be traumatizing to relive what happened to you, so he'll explain the process before you're required to go on record," Stormy said, her tone irritating in its helpfulness.

"Great," I said. "I guess we wait. Thanks for the tea." I slumped down on the sofa.

"Do you want to talk about anything?" Stormy asked.

"I do not."

I was cut off by a knock at the door.

Ice-cold fear gripped me. I threw a glance at Stormy. "Can't be Titanic. Not yet." What if Diving Bill had a partner? What if this wasn't over? What if his 'boss' was on the other side of the door?

Stormy held her finger up to her lips and tiptoed to the door.

She looked through the peephole.

Then she threw the door open wide and shouted, "Grist Featherweight! What're you doing here?"

"Freezing," he answered. "Can I come in?"

Chapter Thirty-Eight

Waggery danced on his perch as I dashed across the living room to Grist. I wrapped my arms around him and started to cry.

"There, there," he said, patting my back. "I knew you'd probably missed me, but I didn't think it would be this bad."

"Oh, Grist," I said through my sobs. "A coroner tried to murder me."

Waggery flew to Grist's shoulder. "Mwah," he said, giving him a kiss.

"Why don't we all have a seat," Stormy suggested. "I'll put another kettle on."

I'd almost forgotten Stormy was in the room. Grist, my Magician card, was here, and I was ready to tell him everything and ready for him to tell me everything was going to be okay.

Waggery remained gripped to Grist's shoulder as we took a seat on the sofa. "Why are you here?" I asked. "I mean, I want you here. I was going to call you. But your honeymoon. And where's Lillian?"

"Sadly, we had to return early," he said. "Because of Lillian's sister."

"Reese?" I asked. "What happened?"

I'd met Reese briefly at Grist and Lillian's wedding. It was a small, potluck affair at Grist's cottage on the Hoggarty Heaven estate. The entire event only lasted a few hours. The happy couple boarded a plane that night and that was that.

It had been a difficult day. I'd been happy Grist and Lillian had found each other. Lillian was keen on keeping Stormy and me close, like family. But the vibes had felt off. And I couldn't stop thinking about Aunt Inez.

Inez and Grist had never married. Was it because Inez had died before they'd had a chance to tie the knot? Or had Lillian, who made moves on Grist quickly after Inez died, pushed for marriage? I didn't get answers before, during, or after the wedding, and I was preoccupied. All I remembered about Reese was that she was friendly and looked a lot like Lillian.

"We're not sure," he said. "Lillian and she are close. When Reese stopped returning her calls, Lillian insisted we fly home. We rested a little to shake off the jet lag, and now we're here. Lillian is at her sister's house right now. She dropped me off here."

"Why aren't you with her?" I asked.

"Good question," he said. The way he slumped when he answered made me think he wasn't happy about it. "I wanted to be there with her, but she said she wanted to handle it on her own. We fought the whole way here about it. But when she said she'd bring me to you, I agreed."

"Wait, Lillian has a sister in Mariner's Cove?" Stormy asked. "Carrie, did you know this?"

"I think Reese may have mentioned she lived on the coast at the wedding, but it didn't register," I said. "Coastal doesn't necessarily mean Mariner's Cove."

Grist took a sip of tea.

"Looks like I arrived at the right time," he continued. "What's this about someone trying to kill you?"

My concern for Lillian and her sister immediately took a back seat as I poured out my thoughts to Grist. Stormy made tea, poured more tea, and cleared the tea away, all while I told Grist the unvarnished truth about the events since I'd arrived in Mariner's Cove.

I told him about everything except the map. I still wasn't sure if I wanted Stormy to know I had it.

When I finished, Stormy remained silent—a noticeable choice since I hadn't minced words with Grist about how she'd been behaving. Grist let out a low whistle.

He shot Stormy a look. "Is this all true?"

She half-nodded and shrugged.

"I can't help but think Inez would be deeply distressed by this turn of events, especially since it indirectly involves her and her work with Ravenous Partners," he said. "All she wanted was for Prosperity to thrive. Then, folks got greedy, she got out, and the whole thing seems to have gone to hell."

I leaned in, ready to ask questions, when there was another knock at the door.

Stormy got up. "I rarely had visitors before, but two weeks with Carrie and my loft has turned into Grand Central Station," she said.

Officer Maigret stood in the doorway, and behind him, her eyes red from crying, was Lillian. And behind her, towering, was Titanic.

"Ms. Portwood," Officer Maigret began. "May I come in? I'd like to speak with you and Ms. Dettwiler."

Lillian wailed.

Grist hurried to her. "What's happened, my darling?"

I cringed a little to hear him call her 'darling.'

"Reese is missing," she said. "A missing person."

Chapter Thirty-Nine

Grist and Lillian huddled in a corner. He consoled; she sobbed. Stormy looked as if she wanted to disappear into the wall. Waggery was back on his perch, snoozing without a care in the world. And Officer Maigret stood before me, ready to make his case.

"Mr. Fitzwilliam was arrested and booked on attempted murder charges and more for you and Ms. Caracatiță. No bond. You're safe from him for now, and between me and the pirates, you are secure."

"What do you mean the pirates?" I asked.

"I've stationed two bodyguards at the entrance to Think Ink," Titanic said. "One of them is Scurvy Doug, who was released about an hour ago. Says he owes you."

I wanted to run to him, thank him, apologize to him, do whatever it took to make this right, even though I still wasn't clear on whose fault any of this was.

"Very kind of you," I said. "It's been a harrowing day. Now this, with Lillian's sister."

"I can't comment," said Officer Maigret. "But I can take your statement on what happened at The Shipwrecks."

I looked at Titanic.

"It's fine, Carrie," he said. "I'm acting as your attorney, but Officer Maigret has already taken my statement, and is working through the rest of the marauders to get their input. Simply tell the truth. You aren't in any trouble."

"Titanic, you told me never to talk to the police," Stormy said, a nerd trying to fit in with the cool kids.

"That particular suggestion is meant for you, Stormy," he said with a hint of a smirk. "Carrie here has nothing to hide."

I gave Officer Maigret my statement, leaving nothing out: Stormy's illegal gun, the car ride, my fear of losing Waggery, and news about the rings.

When I mentioned the treasure, I passed it off like the ravings of a mad killer. There was no benefit to mentioning the credible existence of a treasure in front of all these people.

I handed Officer Maigret the scarf.

"This was almost a murder weapon," I said. "Too bad. It's quite beautiful."

"The knitting needles? The gun?" Officer Maigret asked. "Do you know where those items are?"

"The knitting needles, no," I said. "Lost in the kerfuffle, no doubt. Stormy threw the gun into the ocean."

I could see Stormy shrinking out of the corner of my eye.

"Dumb," he said, shaking his head. "I thought you were smarter, Ms. Portwood. I may need to discuss this further with you, but for now, I'll get a team to go out and find it. If it washes up and someone gets it, you could be held liable."

"You're right, Officer," she said, putting on her most innocent face. "I made a bad decision. I regret it. If you want me to come help, I'll be glad to do so."

"I hope you maintain such a good attitude while you're doing community service. Not sure I can let this go unpunished."

After Officer Maigret left, we all stared at the floor until Grist broke the silence.

"What's next?" Grist asked. "For all of us? Sounds like you have two complicated cases on your hands."

Lillian had stopped crying. Her eyes burned hot red, but her skin was sallow. She sank into herself, her shoulders rounded, as if she were trying to hide.

Lillian ran to Stormy's kitchen and threw up in the trash can.

"Oh, no," Waggery said. He made a sound like gagging. I made a motion for him to be quiet. He blew a raspberry, flew to his perch, and settled in for more napping.

I went to her. "Lillian, I'm so sorry about Reese. When was the last time you heard from her? Is there anything at all I can do to help?"

"No, there's nothing you can do," she said, her words like little bites. "We should go now. Grist? Let's move."

Sweet, soft-spoken Lillian of the Aqua Net and White Diamonds. Lillian, who'd nursed my aunt as she was dying. Grist's wife, whom he married because of her loving eyes, patient demeanor, excellent cooking, and (possible) ultimatum. She was talking like she wanted to rip my head off and was barking orders to Grist.

I was floored.

She huffed past me and opened the door to Stormy's flat, letting a chilly gust of wind in, ruffling the papers on the coffee table, and causing Waggery to shout, "No touching," in his sleep.

I caught Grist's eye despite the fact he was doing his best to avoid looking at my face.

"What?" I mouthed. "Is this?"

He gave me a peck on the cheek. "We'll check in soon."

A chill settled in my spine. "How about we light a fire?" I said, breaking the awkward silence.

Stormy said nothing and got to work on the fire.

"What does one do, Titanic," I began, "when one has nearly been murdered and is otherwise in total life chaos? What do I do now?"

"As your attorney, I would tell you to talk to as few people as possible. Let the facts of the case arise. Stay in town."

"As my friend?"

"I'd tell you to book a trip to Tahiti." His words were joyless. "Otherwise, I'll let you two get back to it. We'll stay in close touch, okay?"

"Aye, aye," I said, closing the door behind him.

I heard a light knock. I opened the door slightly, only enough to hear Titanic whisper, "Careful, Carrie."

Chapter Forty

I became aware of how tired and hungry I was, but I brushed it off. I was ready to get some answers from Stormy.

Seemed Stormy had the same idea.

"My first question for you," Stormy began, "Is where were you going this morning?"

"I'm sorry? Your first question for *me*? Hilarious."

Waggery chuckled.

"You can't bail now, Dettwiler," she said. "We're both in too deep."

Rage threatened to break my brain in half.

"You—," I said breathlessly. "You abandoned me. And, worse, you abandoned Waggery. Where in the hell have you been? Staying out all night? Why do you think I'd tolerate being treated this way?"

"I lost track of time, but there's a reason," she said.

"I know," I said. "I know all about it."

She breathed a sigh of relief. "Amazing," she said. "Then let's get to work."

"Get to work? What, are you two planning a wedding?"

She took a step back.

"Wait—What are you talking about?"

"You and the gray ghost? Or should I say your ex-girlfriend? I saw you hugging in a park. You were so involved you didn't notice your current girlfriend running all over town chasing a pack of wild dogs."

"I'm sorry, what happened? My ex—?"

"Exactly," I said.

"Are you okay?" Stormy appeared genuinely confused.

"I'm most definitely not okay," I said, my voice breaking. "How could you?"

"How could I *what*?"

"Cheat on me. Lie to me." I wanted to accuse her of trying to steal the treasure, but the thought was too heartrending. Stormy had an odd way of moving through the world, but her stealing from me was unthinkable.

"I think you need to lie down. Lie down and let me tell you a story."

I had the urge to fight, scream, yell, and kick over a trash can. But instead, I sank into her sofa and closed my eyes.

I wanted everything to stop.

"The red-haired lady is not who you think she is," Stormy began. "She's not my ex-girlfriend."

I'd heard enough. I sat up. "She's your current girlfriend."

"Carrie, stop. Let me explain."

"C'mon, Waggery. We're going to stay with Grist and Lillian. I'd rather be with my not-uncle and his wife who's in a crisis than listen to how my girlfriend and her new girlfriend are plotting to steal my treasure."

"Whatever you just said is not a thing, Carrie," Stormy said. "We need to talk about the treasure."

Waggery sensed my ire and flew to my shoulder. The car was already packed. All I had to do was figure out where Lillian and Grist were staying.

"Goodbye, Stormy," I said and closed the door behind me.

Chapter Forty-One

Waggery sat on my lap purring, as I cried in the car.

"Sorry you have to see me like this," I said.

"Poor Carrie," he said in Aunt Inez's voice. I started to sob again.

Time was passing, and the temperature was dropping. Might as well get myself to wherever Grist and Lillian were staying as soon as possible. Maybe Lillian had cookies. Lillian always had cookies.

Grist texted the address with a note saying Lillian wasn't herself and we should lie low. Perfect. The only thing on my current agenda was to lie low.

I wasn't going far, and, in my rush, I wasn't able to negotiate Waggery into his crate. I explained the situation to him, and he seemed to understand. He sat placidly on the three-minute drive as I piloted Grist's car into the hills. I spotted Lillian's Camry in a driveway.

"Oh, no," Waggery said.

"Oh, no is right, Wags," I said as I pulled in.

Despite the fear making my face tingle, I had to see for myself. I had to know.

"Stay right here, okay, Wags?"

I exited the car and walked slowly up the path. The solar-powered lights flickered on.

Grist opened the door.

"Welcome, Carrie. You find it okay?"

I nodded.

He stepped out of the way.

I walked through the door.

I was standing in Baba Caracatiţă's living room.

"Why are you staying here?" I asked. "In this house?"

Lillian emerged from the back, wearing a robe and drying her hair with a towel.

"Carrie! What are you doing here?"

She dropped the towel.

"This is Reese's, Lillian's sister's, home," Grist said in a gentle tone. "We're pleased to have you here. But you can understand this is a difficult time."

"It is a difficult time," I repeated. "Yeah. Yes. Okay. You know what? I'm going to go get Waggery from the car. And settle in. I'll stay out of your freshly washed hair."

I backed out of the door.

"Be right back," I said.

I ran to the car, opened the door, climbed in, and drove away as fast as I could, leaving a confused Grist standing on Baba's front porch, framed in my rearview mirror like a photograph.

Chapter Forty-Two

Oh, no.

I didn't know who knew what, who to tell what, where to go, or whether to hide.

I stopped the car downtown in front of the police station.

Was I supposed to go in?

What would I say, exactly?

Could I go back to Stormy's? Was she in on this?

Was Grist?

What was the next right thing?

Whom could I trust?

Only one answer presented itself: Titanic Jones.

* * *

I arrived at his office after dark, carrying a raven on one shoulder and a chip on the other.

I must've looked a mess because when he saw me, he stood up, walked over, and embraced me. Waggery hopped on to his shoulder and gave him a kiss.

"You poor thing," he said. "You've got way too much drama for one person to deal with."

I spilled everything. The map. Stormy's cheating. The secret of the three rings. I wasn't sure what he knew and what he didn't, so I kept talking until he stopped me.

"Enough," he said. "We have loose threads, but we can tie them up. Let me start, okay?"

"Fine," I said. "Any help I can get, assuming you aren't a member of a secret cabal trying to murder me."

"Fortunately, I am not," he said. "First things first. Let's get you and Stormy in a room together. She's not cheating."

"What are you saying? You're the one who's Whisper McWhisperson, telling me to be careful between closing doors. And the redhead!"

"More than one redhead in the world," he said. "When I cautioned you to be careful, I was talking about Lillian."

The edges of my vision blurred, and I thought I might pass out. "Oh," was all I could muster.

Because I knew it was true.

"Is Stormy in danger?"

"I don't know," he said. "There's safety in numbers, so let's corral all of these rings, maps, papers, whatever... into one room. I'm taking you back to Stormy's."

"Would you mind taking Waggery with you? He could use the fresh air, and I don't want to put him back in the car."

"Saddle up, me Hearty," Titanic said.

Waggery hopped onto Titanic's shoulder like he'd done it a thousand times. "Mwah."

I watched as they walked through the streets of Mariner's Cove, looking for all the world like a murder pirate and his grisly familiar.

Spike was outside when I pulled into a space in front of Think Ink.

"I saw Titanic with your chicken!" he said.

"It's after dark, Spike," I said, with no attempt to hide the weariness in my voice. "Shouldn't you be at home?"

I wanted to tell him how his floor is lava game helped save my life, but I would have to save the story for another day.

"Go home," I said. "There's a murderer on the loose."

"You mean like Assassin? Stormy said I'm too young to play. Stormy's mean."

"Kind of. Please go home and stay safe."

He turned to go.

"Spike?" I called behind him. "Did you get your dog back?"

"What dog?" he called back.

"I don't have an answer," I said, thinking I'd been lied to again.

"Oh yeah," he said. "We do have a dog."

Bored with me, Spike bounded down the street and out of sight.

Was there any end to the strangeness of this place?

I took the stairs two at a time and arrived in Stormy's apartment to find Titanic, Waggery, Stormy, and a redhead waiting for me.

"Whoa," I said.

Stormy stepped forward. "I'm so happy you're back. I was worried."

I let her hug me, but only responded weakly.

"I want you to meet someone."

"Gray Ghost," I said, waiting for the bad news.

"This is Cecily."

I waited.

"It's nice to meet you, Carrie," Cecily said. "Finally."

She and Stormy locked eyes. They knew each other.

"Why have you been following me?" I asked.

"I haven't, exactly," she said. "I've been looking for my ring.

We happened to cross paths a few times, but I wasn't techni-cally following you."

My eyes bubbled with tears. "Are you all—are you going to kill me now? For the treasure?"

My eyes shot to Waggery, who hopped up and down on Titanic's shoulder.

"Never," Stormy said. "I know things seem suspicious, but we can explain everything."

"I can't believe I'm speaking to you," Cecily said. "I'm over-whelmed."

I saw a few tears escape and roll down her cheeks.

"What's going on? I'm so tired. Will someone please explain what I'm involved in here?"

Silence.

"No one? No one's going to fill me in? As usual?"

"I'll fill you in," Stormy said. "You may want to sit."

"I'm not a child. Tell me."

Titanic motioned for Stormy to speak. He looked at his hands.

"Cecily is technically our captive," Stormy began.

My eyes darted to Cecily's hands. She wasn't tied up. "Really? Looks like she's a regular person. No cuffs? No zip ties?"

Stormy ignored me. "When Titanic and I realized she was looking for the rings, we believed she was a danger to you. I enlisted the help of the pirates, and we kidnapped her. She's been our hostage ever since."

I was unable to form words.

"Cecily is after our rings. And it took some stern treatment, but Titanic and I finally got an answer out of her."

Cecily took a step forward. "I tried to tell them I only want the rings. Mine, specifically. I don't want to hurt anyone."

"We thought she might have killed Baba," Titanic said.

"The best course of action was to keep her away from you until we were satisfied by her answers and explanations. We treated her well; not a hair on her head was harmed."

"That's true," Cecily confirmed. "The quietest kidnapping ever, but I'm still put out by it. I'm not a danger to anyone."

"Then why are you here?" I asked.

"I believe Ravenous Partners killed my parents. And from what Stormy shared about what you both have been through, I think they might have killed yours."

§

When Mom and Dad told me I'd be staying at Aunt Inez's for a few days while they went on a vacation, I ran out of the kitchen, dashed down the hall to my room, and started packing.

I couldn't wait.

I'd spent the night at her house before, but this visit was going to be five whole nights of me, Aunt Inez's boyfriend Grist, and Waggery, who was beginning to warm up to me, despite the fact I was an over-curious ten-year-old. I'd discovered if I brought him raw, unsalted peanuts in the shell, he forgave me for not being Inez. She was his favorite person, to the exclusion of most everyone else. I could hardly blame him; I felt the same way about her.

My memory of my parents leaving town was hazy. I stood under Aunt Inez's mimosa tree, making faces at Waggery, while Mom told me she'd miss me, said I needed to behave, and they'd be back soon. Dad was getting antsy, wanting to beat traffic, the way dads do. Mom kneeled down, kissed my forehead, and told me not to bother Waggery so much.

Nothing out of the ordinary.

Waking up in Aunt Inez's house on a sunny summer

morning was its own special treat. Her guest room was bright and tidy, with crisp, line-dried cotton sheets. She'd leave the window open all night so the room would be cool enough for me to feel comfy under heavy quilts, and to allow the smell of her abundant star jasmine to fill the space. I'd laughed myself silly at Grist's jokes and Waggery's antics before bed, so sleep was deep and refreshing.

I would emerge earlier than I normally woke up and in a better mood, simply because I couldn't wait to see Aunt Inez and Waggery.

And have Inez make me breakfast, of course.

Eggs from the neighbors' chickens, cooked to perfection, with thick bacon, toast from home-baked bread and an ever-changing lineup of seasonal berries and fruit. I was hoping for white peaches, which were hanging heavy and ripe from the trees she'd planted decades ago.

I stretched and took a deep breath. Inhaled the heavy, too-sweet liquor of the flowers waking up outside. Told myself this was going to be a great day. The town of Prosperity was building a public duck pond and Aunt Inez was going to show me where.

Funny, though. I didn't smell bacon.

Aunt Inez had the cutest robe for me hanging on the back of the door. I put it on and stepped out into the main part of the house.

Grist was there. Fully dressed in his work clothes, which meant he was wearing a top hat and silk vest to resemble town founder Agustus Hoggarty. Grist was a tour guide, among other things. But he looked out of place sitting at the kitchen table.

Aunt Inez was still in her clothes from the day before.

She startled when she saw me. "Carrie," she said. "Did you sleep well? Have a seat."

I began to suspect I wasn't getting white peaches.

Waggery watched me but didn't make a sound.

I took a seat.

"What's wrong?" I asked. "Am I in trouble?"

Aunt Inez sat down. She took my hands in hers.

"Carrie, my darling. There's been an accident."

The next several weeks were a blur. Aunt Inez and Grist made furiously fast work of getting me set up to live in Prosperity. I didn't have to lift a finger or move a thing. It was magic. All my stuff simply appeared at her house.

We immediately dove into tarot lessons. Looking back, I'm certain this was Aunt Inez's way of coping. I'm grateful to her for keeping my mind busy and active. I was fine when we took Waggery for walks, taught him tricks, studied tarot, worked in her garden, made food, and entertained guests, but during down times—dark thoughts crept in.

This isn't to say Aunt Inez and I ignored our grief. We cried together. We shared memories. She lifted me up on my bad days. I lifted her up on hers.

We were honest and open with each other, or so I thought. Until I told her a secret. Her reaction to my revelation was the only crack in our relationship.

"Aunt Inez," I began one night we were both feeling gloomy. "Mom said something to me before she left."

She took off her glasses. "Oh? Why didn't you tell me before?"

"I just remembered now," I said. "She told me she had a surprise for me when she came back."

The color drained from Aunt Inez's face. "Do you have any idea what she meant?"

I didn't, and I assumed Aunt Inez thought I was trying to get a present out of her, so I changed the subject.

"No," I said. "I remembered, is all."

She put her glasses back on and went back to whatever she was doing. "Probably best if we don't think about those things."

I never mentioned it again.

§

Chapter Forty-Three

Camila and Jason Dettwiler, my parents, told everyone they were headed for a long weekend at Lake Liminal. The kind of easy vacation no one would question. Of course the young couple wanted a weekend away for themselves. It was only natural.

It was a car accident. Dark night. Fallen tree. Nothing special about the story as far as I knew.

I still grieve, but the pain is different now. Less acute. Aunt Inez's death re-opened those wounds, but Grist had done the job of a whole family in bringing me back from the dark, all while he was mourning the loss of his beloved partner.

I didn't like to talk about any of this. I especially didn't like my private story, my personal pain, being brought up by a stranger who I believed had been chasing me.

"Thank you so much, both of you, for playing the greatest hits of Carrie's trauma. I feel great about everything."

I know I sounded bitter but I didn't care.

Stormy looked alarmed. "Hey, Carrie, it's okay. No one's trying to hurt you."

I rolled my eyes. "No one ever wants to hurt Carrie, but

here we are. My girlfriend and her new girlfriend are manipulating me with some made-up story. Total fantasy. Oh, but thank you for not wanting to hurt me. Just club me on the head, steal the rings, ride off into the sunset."

"Oh, no," Waggery said.

The room went wobbly. Objects swam. The edges of my vision blackened.

"She's panicking," I heard Stormy say.

"Get her some juice. And protein." I heard a voice say.

I flopped onto the sofa. Waggery flew to the coffee table to get closer to me.

I left my body. I didn't know when I was going to return.

* * *

The following morning, I was still on the sofa. Someone had given me a pillow and propped my feet up. I was under heavy blankets and feeling so cozy...

Until I remembered.

I closed my eyes again, hoping to go back in time to before any of this happened.

Waggery snored on the armrest.

I heard someone in the kitchen behind me.

Cecily.

"I made you some tea," she said and sat by my feet.

"How long was I out?" I asked.

"Looks like about twelve hours," she said. "You needed it. I've seen you. You've been on a wild goose chase."

"I have," I said. I leaned in to get the teacup and took a sip. It tasted like nectar.

"I don't mean to push," she said. "We have a lot to do, and we have to work quickly."

"Where have you and Stormy been going? Why all the secrecy? Were you intentionally leaving me out?"

"No, not at all. Stormy caught me breaking and entering, and things got intense from there."

"You broke into Think Ink and left a note," I said,

"I broke into Think Ink trying to find my ring," she said. "The note was a demand letter, but she didn't come to the meeting place. She told Titanic instead. When you spotted me on Slithering Eel, she unleashed a horde of pirates after me. It was kind of terrifying. I think it was supposed to be."

"Stormy can be scary. I have to ask. Did you murder Baba?"

"Of course not, and that's what I told Stormy. She thought I was lying. She told me to leave town immediately. I refused. I needed to see you. I needed my ring back. She was monkeying up the works. That's when they said they weren't letting me go."

"You're awfully calm about all of this."

"I told them they could hold me hostage. I wasn't going anywhere. Not until I met you. I wanted the three of us together so we could discuss what we knew about these emerald rings. One of them is mine. I want it back as badly as you want yours back. But I'm not willing to murder over it.

"Mind you, it was the kindest kidnapping ever," she continued. "Titanic made sandwiches. They asked me things. Took turns not believing me. They finally untied me because the whole felony kidnapping thing made them uncomfortable. I didn't escape. I stayed. And then they began to trust me."

The fog of first awakening was wearing off, and I was starting to feel weird about this conversation. "Let's talk more when Stormy wakes up," I said. "I want to make sure your stories match."

"Fine," she said. "That's exactly what I want. I have something to tell both of you."

I wasn't willing to wait. I went to Stormy's room and shook her awake.

"Portwood. Now."

"Aye, aye," she said, her voice scratchy.

Cecily was standing in the living room as if she were about to make a speech. I took a seat. Stormy flopped beside me, dressed in her terry robe, and yawned.

"I guess we have a lot to discuss," she said.

Cecily began. "I was raised in Sacramento by a single mother named Katrina Cascada. Does that ring a bell?"

It didn't, and we both shook our heads.

"Cascada? As in Teresa Cascada?"

"That's Baba's real name," I said. "Are you saying you're related to Baba?"

"Teresa is my aunt. You know her as Baba. I've been coming to Mariner's Cove to visit for years. It's how I know my way around."

"Oh, my," I said, as it came together. I saw the players dance before my eyes like a card spread.

"Teresa," I said. "She goes by 'Reese?'"

Cecily nodded.

I felt as if a hole in the center of my body was expanding. "Teresa Cascada is your mother's sister. She is also known as Baba and she goes by Reese to her family. That means that Lillian, Grist's wife, is your other aunt."

"Baba was trying to protect you, Carrie. She knew you and Stormy were here with your rings, and she told me it was time to come for mine. She was going to help us. She took your ring because she thought she could hide it for you, for us. If you didn't have it on your person, no one would kill you for it. She was going to explain all of it and then—." Cecily looked down.

I was reeling from the information I was receiving, but now I realized how much Cecily had lost, too. My compassion for her overflowed, and I thought it was too much to ask her to continue.

Unfortunately, we didn't have such luxury. I straightened my back and pressed on.

"How did she get yours, and the map?"

"Inez had already sent the bloodhound antiques dealer, LeMarcus, after it before she died. Lillian primed Inez for info, so she could credibly tell LeMarcus it was Inez's wish for Reese to get the rings and the map. Lillian had plans for her and her sister to steal our rings, the map, and the treasure. But my Aunt Teresa—Reese—Baba threatened to reveal the plan. She told me the rings belonged to you, me, and Stormy and no one else, and she was determined to keep it that way. Now she's dead."

"How devastating for you," I said. "I'm so sorry about your loss."

"Thank you," she said. "I need to get this next bit of news out. It's about Lillian."

"Lillian," I repeated, having difficulty controlling my breath. "What about her?" My skin prickled.

"It's her," Cecily said.

"What are you talking about?"

"Lillian is the mastermind. She hired Diving Bill. She knows her sister is dead, and she's pretending she's missing. Diving Bill has been feeding her information."

I held up a hand for Cecily to please stop talking. Nothing in my experience had prepared me to hear the words that Lillian Valli was a mastermind of anything. Other than getting Grist to marry her, of course. But that was Lillian. Romantic. Thoughtful. A bit meek. If I was so wrong about her, what else was I wrong about?

A sickening thought wedged itself into my brain.

Grist.

"Grist? Is he...? Is he involved?"

I didn't think I could continue living if I believed Grist was trying to murder me.

Stormy's eyes were wide. Her skin looked waxy. I don't think she understood what she was hearing, either. She knew all the players, but she knew them as I did: oddball, surrogate parents who loved to feed us and give advice. Not co-conspirators.

Certainly not murderers.

"Lillian loves Grist," Cecily said. "I don't believe he's in immediate danger, not like you are. But, Carrie—"

"No more news," I said. "No more. I can't."

"Lillian hired William Fitzwilliam to murder her sister and then you and Stormy. She also poisoned your Aunt Inez."

"What—"

"It was the broth, Carrie."

"No." This was impossible.

"I'm so sorry, Carrie, but it's true."

Broth.

The broth.

I grabbed Stormy's hand and held on for dear life. She winced but didn't let go.

The 'healing' broth was the only nourishment Aunt Inez could tolerate at the end. I had spooned it into her mouth, and it had killed her.

"How?" This was all I could squeak out.

"Lilies."

I felt dizzy. "Lillian put lilies on her tray because I told her Aunt Inez loved them. Every time she visited, it was broth and a lily. Oh, God." I started to shake.

"Carrie, this isn't your fault." Cecily's voice was urgent. "She used the lily bulbs as if they were onions, and the cardiac glycosides poisoned Inez over time."

I wanted to scream and burn Mariner's Cove and everyone in it to the ground.

"I'm so sorry, Carrie," Stormy said, her voice trembling. "Is there anything we can do for you?"

Everything was fuzzy. I couldn't focus. "I can't believe you kidnapped someone, Stormy. What the hell?" My voice sounded far away, as if someone else were speaking through me.

"Hey, I used your buddy Hank's playbook. He kidnapped me and left me in a tunnel beneath a burning building."

"What—" Cecily began.

"Water under the bridge. It's all good now, right, Carrie?"

"Oh, no, it wasn't terrible at all, Carrie," Cecily said. "I wanted them on my side, so I agreed to stay out of the way until they could confirm we were related. I needed a place to stay because I couldn't be seen at Reese's house. Titanic's place is very comfortable, and he was a perfect gentleman. It worked out."

"No, it didn't," I said. "I don't believe you."

"I think she's telling the truth, Carrie."

"I refuse to accept this." I stood up and stomped around the room. "I don't know her. I didn't 'kidnap' her. I don't trust her. Lillian didn't kill Inez. I can't believe that. Ever. And that Grist may be a part of it? Absolutely not. Never. No."

I was as angry as I'd ever been. Waggery scurried under the coffee table as I raged around the room.

"I have a plan," Cecily said. "Your anger is justified. I'm raging, too. And I know that Stormy is none too pleased. Let's figure out, together, what the truth is. We'll do that by taking this to the top. We're going straight to Lillian."

Cecily chattered about 'cornering' and 'confessions' as she sketched out a rough plan.

Stormy seemed on board, enthusiastic.

I continued to reel from my new reality. "With one caveat," I said. "Stormy and I confront Lillian, not you."

"Why not?" Cecily sounded stung.

"Two reasons. One, if you're telling the truth, she's going to know something is amiss if you walk in. Two, if you're lying, I don't want you there. Period."

"I'll stay in the car."

"Will that work for you, Carrie?" Stormy asked. "I believe her, but I've known her for a few days longer. She'll be there to help, but in the shadows."

"I accept." We all shook hands.

Waggery came out from under the coffee table and said, "Hooray!"

"You know what I really want?" I asked. I could feel stress hives forming on my neck. My anger was hot as a wildfire, and I was ready to be engulfed.

"Anything," Stormy said, looking at me deeply with her gorgeous gray eyes.

"I want Justice."

Chapter Forty-Four

The Justice card can be a welcome sign in a tarot reading. Typically, the querent believes justice will be served on their behalf, not that justice will be served against them. What most people want when they see the Justice card is revenge.

I wanted justice too. I was perilously tipping into a dark territory. My fury, my pain, was so blinding I knew I needed something to keep me sane. And despite our miscommunications, I held fast to Stormy to keep me grounded. Was Cecily my new Justice card? Or was she the Devil the spreads had been warning me about?

We were about to find out.

Stormy and Cecily sat with me, made me tea, dabbed my tears, and gave me hugs while I processed intense emotions.

"Enough," I said, after finally wearing myself out. "We need every detail of the plan in place before we move. Is Grist in danger?" This new thought threatened to paralyze me again, but I tried to stay focused. For Grist.

"Hard to say," Stormy said. "If he doesn't know, then no. If he does know, then probably. And, Carrie—"

"Don't say it," I said. "I can't hear this."

I got up and took my teacup to the sink.

"You must hear it, Carrie. Because it could be true."

I sensed Cecily and Stormy exchanging glances behind my back.

Cecily, new to this dynamic, spoke first. Stormy wouldn't have dared.

"It's possible he's been in on it from the beginning," she said. "It's also possible he has no idea."

"Let's call the police and let them sort it out," I said. "Maybe that's the best plan. Let the chips, or rings in this case, fall where they may."

"I thought of calling the police," Stormy said. "But I want to protect Grist. He'll be a suspect if we turn Lillian in. We need to talk to him first."

"How? She won't let him be alone with me."

"I can't exactly pop in, as you surmised correctly before," Cecily said. "Lillian doesn't know about my involvement. She thinks I'm sitting in Sacramento."

"Right," Stormy said. "Your presence would spook her. And with everything going on, she'd be on high alert if I showed up alone for no reason."

"She's still pretending she doesn't know what happened to her sister," I said, shuddering. "What kind of psychopath knows their sister is dead and lets law enforcement continue to look for her like she's a missing person?"

"If Reese is still missing, she's not legally dead," Cecily said. "No body. No crime. Lillian is buying time by sending the cops on a snipe hunt."

"You have a dark side, Cecily," I said. "The whole Baba thing is going to come out, right?"

"Definitely. Especially since Diving Bill is in custody and

looking to throw blame. We have to corner Lillian as soon as possible."

"I have an idea," I said. "Get Titanic on the phone."

* * *

We'd hatched a plan. Cecily went to Titanic's house for some rest, leaving Stormy and me alone.

"How could you keep these things from me for so long?" My voice had risen and continued to do so. "You had no right. No right to leave me here, freezing to death, struggling to sort this out while you were meeting—or should I say *kidnapping*—people behind my back and not even bothering to check in with me."

Waggery, unaccustomed to shouting, scurried into Stormy's bedroom, only peeking his head out every few minutes to make sure we were still alive.

"What are you madder about?" Stormy asked. "The kidnapping, or the lack of communication?"

"Don't deflect, Portwood. I'm furious about all of it."

"I thought it would be best if I didn't lie to you. So, I didn't lie. I disappeared instead."

"You're suspicious all the time," I said. "What's it going to take for you to see things from my point of view? Can you understand why I'm upset?"

"Because you missed me?"

The urge to stomp out was powerful. But I knew her defense mechanisms, and I wasn't going to let her push me away. Not until she listened to me.

"Stormy," I began, "I'm in love with you. I want a life with you. But not if you keep running off and losing touch with me. I thought you were cheating on me with Cecily! All this time, I believed you were sneaking around with her while I was trying to find my ring, help Scurvy Doug, and keep Waggery safe. I needed you. I needed my partner, and she was—with someone else."

Stormy sat down.

"Can you see why I'd think that you and Cecily were up to no good?" I asked.

When she finally looked at me, her face was pale, and her eyes were wet.

"Carrie, I need you to know something."

My neck prickled. I braced for bad news.

"I hear you," she said, not breaking eye contact. "I understand what you're saying. I've never had to check in with anyone. I've never had to consider another person's feelings before. This relationship thing is new to me, too."

"You've had girlfriends before, Stormy."

"Not like you," she said quickly. "I've never had feelings like this. I've never been in love like this."

"Stormy, I—"

"Let me finish. I fully accept my actions looked suspicious to you. But to me? Everything I was doing, I was doing for you."

My back tensed. I was ready to defend myself. "*For* me?"

"In my brain, I was solving the puzzle for you. I was protecting you from danger. Protecting you from Cecily. I was your savior, your hero, your knight in shining armor. I fully imagined sweeping in to save the day so my beautiful Carrie could continue to heal after everything she's gone through. The last thing I wanted was for you to suffer. And apparently, you suffered anyway. I can't lose you. I love you. More than anything."

I wanted to hold onto my anger. I wanted to make her feel my pain. But I understood Stormy. I knew the answer to who hurt her, who made her feel she had to sneak around, who treated her as if she wasn't trustworthy. Her father had given her these abandonment issues. He'd been one of my closest friends.

"I'm sorry, Carrie. I am. Please, don't hate me."

"I don't hate you, Stormy, when you do things like this. The sneaking. The skulking. The dipping out without an explanation. Can you see how none of your behavior makes me hate you? It makes me hate myself."

Her hand went to her face as if I'd punched her.

"When you behave this way," I continued, "I feel like I'm not worthy of being included. I'm not lovable enough to be a priority."

Her face softened. "I see it now. I'm so unspeakably sorry."

"Sorry for hurting me, or sorry for getting caught?"

"If it helps, I always knew I'd get caught. But I thought you'd understand. Our whole vibe is opposites who understand each other."

I did understand.

"Stormy, promise you won't run off anymore."

"I don't need to run off anymore," she said. "Everything's out on the table."

"Not the point!"

"Carrie, you're so tired. And so cold. You're shivering."

I hadn't noticed, but she was right.

"Sit down. Have this blanket. I have a present for you." She made a big show of tucking the blanket all around me, leaving my arms out. I looked like a half-done mummy. Or a cold-climate mermaid.

Stormy returned, bearing a large, rectangular box topped with a black, camel, and red plaid bow.

She placed it on my lap.

"Open it," she said.

I pulled the top off slowly and gently removed the tissue paper.

The contents were so heavy I had to sit up straight.

"Lift from your core," Stormy said with a twinkle in her eye.

It was a coat.

I threw off the blanket and stood up to try it on.

I spun around a few times. "What do you think?"

"It's cashmere," she said. "I don't think you'll be cold anymore."

I ran my hands over the fabric.

"It's gray," I said. "Fitting."

"Total coincidence," she said. "I'm not trying to bribe you. I bought this before I knew you were mad. See the shoulder?"

A quilted patch was attached to the left shoulder of the coat.

"I had them custom make a removable patch for Waggery to dig his claws into. So the whole thing doesn't get ruined."

At the sound of his name, Waggery poked his head out of the bedroom, saw nothing interesting, and settled onto the floor with a human-sounding sigh.

I'm not one to be dazzled by expensive gifts, but I was touched by Stormy's gesture. I couldn't believe how warm I finally was.

"It's gorgeous," I said. "So toasty. Thank you. It's officially the nicest thing I own." The fabric was so soft I couldn't stop rubbing it.

"There's more," she said.

"More? This coat is an embarrassment of riches."

"Check the pockets."

I put my hands in the (extremely plush and warm) pockets and pulled out a deck of cards from the right one.

It was the *Regina Tentaculelor*.

"I can't take this. It's stolen."

I flipped through the cards; each one was more beautiful than the last.

"Cecily and I talked about it during the 'kidnapping,'" she

said, making quotation marks in the air. "She agreed you should have them. As for the rest of Baba's collection, she's working with LeMarcus to liquidate, unless there's anything else you want."

"This is way more than enough. Baba's items should find homes with people who appreciate them. Of course, this is probably one of her most valuable finds. I can't imagine there are too many more of these decks out there."

"Do you know what *Regina Tentaculelor* translates to?"

"It means 'queen of tentacles' in Romanian'" I said. "In English, it's a pun. Aren't they gorgeous? Thank you so much, Stormy."

"You're welcome," she said. "I'll do whatever you ask, anything you want to make it up to you. I refuse to lose you. You're my person."

"So. you weren't trying to cheat on me with a mysterious stranger from Sacramento?"

"I only have eyes for you," she said.

She took my hand in hers, and we sat in silence.

"Besides," she said. "Cecily's straight as an arrow. I was thinking of setting her up with Titanic."

My stomach fluttered. "I love the idea."

"Can we stop fighting now?" she asked.

"Yes," I said. "I know Stormy's gonna Stormy. But try to remember we're a team now. Okay? I need you."

She pulled me close and kissed me. "Carrie Dettwiler, I will never abandon you or lie to you or hide the truth or anything remotely sketchy ever again. This is my solemn vow."

"Then I forgive you," I said. And I did. Our life together had been filled with drama and intrigue, stress, death, and pirates. I couldn't blame her for not knowing how to act in such extreme situations. "Can we cuddle on the couch for a thousand hours now?"

"Not yet."

She got up, walked to the kitchen, pulled a bottle of wine out of the fridge, uncorked it, and poured two tall glasses.

She handed me one and said, "Drink this. You deserve to relax. We have a devious plan. And we need to execute it tomorrow."

Chapter Forty-Five

Turns out Titanic enjoyed a caper. When we explained what we needed, he hopped right to it.

"He's coming," Titanic said when he called us back. "Grist and I are meeting in one hour to tour The Shipwrecks. I'll tell him everything while you corner Lillian. I mean, spend time with her, asking perfectly legal questions in a perfectly legal way with nothing illegal. Got it?"

"Thank you, Titanic," I said. "Be extra gentle with Grist. I believe he's about to be blindsided. And if you feel he was somehow in on it, text me the word 'raven' and we'll shift our plan appropriately."

I couldn't believe I was saying anything about Grist being involved. Stormy and I had been going around about this for hours. I was convinced Grist had been hoodwinked; Stormy thought we should be prepared for everything. She won the argument.

"Aye, aye," Titanic said. "Captain."

Why did that make me smile?

"We have one hour," I told Stormy and Cecily. "We can get Lillian alone and extract a confession. Stormy?"

"Yes, ma'am," she replied.

"You'll record everything on your phone."

"Righty-o."

"Cecily?"

"Yes, Carrie?"

She looked frightened. I reached out and squeezed her hand.

"You're the bombshell hiding in the car until the right moment."

"Understood."

"Waggery, you do you."

"Quok," he agreed.

* * *

We arrived at Baba's home when we were certain Grist was out of the house and in Titanic's charismatic company. If the scenario hadn't been so terrifying, I would have been able to appreciate how much Grist was going to love The Shipwrecks. As it was, I was focused on not peeing myself and ruining my beautiful new coat.

"Let's go serve up some piping hot justice," Stormy said as we walked together toward the front door.

"I know how much you love shenanigans," I said.

Cecily waited in the car. I looked back over my shoulder and gave her the thumbs up. She looked worried. Or as worried as I thought she could look, having only recently met her.

Waggery sat patiently on my shoulder. He, like Stormy, was a crimer, and I could tell he was reveling in being a part of a secret plan.

"You recording?" I whispered to Stormy.

She nodded, not taking her eyes off the door.

I knocked.

There was a commotion on the other side of the door. It sounded like Lillian moving things around, possibly ending a phone call, or talking to herself.

The door opened.

"Stormy! Carrie! Waterloo! I didn't know you were coming."

Seeing her standing there weakened my knees and churned my stomach. I'd never hated anyone, but I imagined this is how hatred would feel. Like a toxic chemical coursing through your veins, poisoning you with every pulse of your heart.

With no time to waste, Stormy stepped right through the door, creating a wide berth for Waggery and I to follow.

"I hope it's not a bad time," Stormy said.

"Titanic mentioned he was taking Grist to The Shipwrecks, so we thought we'd pop by and keep you company," I said, my voice stronger than I thought it would be. I was shaky, but I decided to use my anger to my advantage. "I'm so worried about Reese. You must be beside yourself."

"Yes, um. I am," she said. "It's such a shock."

Stormy had already taken off her jacket and flopped down on the sofa. She picked up a remote. "You have cable. Awesome. You guys wanna watch *Ink Masters?*"

Before a flustered Lillian could respond, I chimed in.

"I brought you a gift." I pulled a thermos filled with Down the Hatch fish stew and placed it on the counter. "Mariner's Cove's top delicacy. Ideal for a gloomy day like this one. Bowls?"

Waggery flew to the top of her television armoire and began grooming himself.

Lillian motioned to a cabinet. I found the bowls and dished up stew.

"You didn't have to do anything special," she said. She fidgeted, as if she wasn't quite sure what to do with her hands.

"Have a seat," I said.

Stormy patted the cushion next to her. "Sit here," she said.

I gave them each a bowl and joined them in the living room.

"This wasn't necessary," she said, spooning some stew into her mouth. "Thank you, girls. It's delicious."

"You are more than welcome, Lillian," I said. Sitting politely across from her, watching her spoon dabs of stew into her tiny mouth, filled me with an unfathomable fury. "You've always been there for me and my family, even in the darkest of times. With food. With love. It's the least I can do."

"Are there any new clues?" Stormy asked. "Any leads on what may have happened to your sister?"

"Nothing yet. Officer Maigret said to be patient," she said. She kept looking over her shoulder. "I'm waiting here in case she returns. I'm kind of stuck. I was glad Grist was able to visit with Titanic, though, seeing as our honeymoon was cut short and all."

"Generous of you," I said.

A knock sounded at the door.

Lillian looked confused.

"Oh, I think I know what this might be," I said, faux giggling. "We have a surprise."

I opened the door.

"Spike!" I said. "I was hoping we'd be here when you came through."

"What is this? What's happening?" Lillian was standing next to me, looking down at Spike, who was holding a stack of flyers.

"Do I need to do the whole thing?" Spike asked in a tone so whiny I thought he might be speaking through his nose.

"Yes, you do!" I said. "Show Lillian what we practiced this morning."

He cleared his throat and stared at the sky as he recited what we had taught him.

"A local woman has gone missing. Please, take these flyers, and if you have any information, call the tip line. There's a reward."

He handed the flyer to Lillian. Centered in black and white was a photocopied image of Teresa in her regular beige clothes.

MISSING PERSON
Teresa Cascada A.K.A. Baba Caracaţia
Call the police with tips and clues.
REWARD: Antique Emerald Ring

"What in the holy heck is this?" Lillian wasn't very good at hiding her panic. Her face turned beet red.

"Can I be done here?" Spike asked. "I've got a metric butt-ton of other houses to get to. I did paper the entire downtown, though."

"Off with you!" I said. "Make sure those posters are *everywhere*."

I closed the door and sat back on the sofa. "People say there are problems with the youth today, but I have to say Spike is a real asset."

"He sure is," Stormy said. "Good kid."

Lillian didn't think we noticed her flitting around the house, chewing her fingers.

"I think these posters will help, don't you, Lillian?" I said.

"How—?"

"How, what, Lil?" I was enjoying myself. It was fun watching her squirm.

"When did you find out about... Baba?"

"It feels like one of those things we've always known, doesn't it, Carrie?" Stormy had a sharp look in her eye.

"Maybe. Everything feels so vague. Trauma upon trauma."

"You girls don't understand what you've done. And what you're up against," Lillian said.

"Why don't you tell us?" I asked. "Stormy, make some popcorn."

Lillian's face changed. I'd never seen her so much as frown, much less contort her face into the kind of sneer usually reserved for horror films. "You ungrateful brat."

"Ouch, Lillian. I brought you stew."

"It was delish, wasn't it, Carrie?" Stormy patted her stomach.

"I didn't eat any," I said. "You didn't really eat it, did you, Stormy?"

"You caught me," she said. "Eating the stew is ill-advised, right, Carrie?"

"I'd say so." I dumped our bowls in the sink. "I'm sure Lil here thinks it's fine."

"What do you mean?" Lillian asked. She looked quickly back and forth between Stormy and me.

"They're using a new broth," I said. "With the exact ingredients from the broth you fed my Aunt Inez."

Saying the words out loud made them true. Lillian had murdered my beloved caretaker, my beautiful Aunt Inez. My upper lip quivered uncontrollably and my throat swelled. But I didn't back down.

"No." Lillian backed away.

I checked my phone. Nothing from Titanic, which let me know Grist was not in on Lillian's horrifying plan.

"How did you find out? About the broth. About any of it?" Lillian had her hand on her heart.

"The broth was so healing for my aunt when she was ill. I only wanted to repay the kindness with kindness."

"You put the lily bulbs in, too?" She asked, her hand at her throat.

"Even if we did, you know a bit of lily juice won't kill you today, don't you? You might have gastric distress, perhaps a palpitation or two. But to properly poison someone without any suspicion takes time. In Aunt Inez's case it took you what? Almost a year?"

Lillian's face was waxy.

"Fortunately for you, Lillian, there aren't many lilies growing in this icebox of a town."

"Righty-o, Carrie," Stormy said. "Not a lily as far as the eye can see. We had to use a different poison. Good old rat poison from the hardware store."

The rat poison was a deviation from the script.

I watched Lillian wobble. "What have you done?"

"Naturally, we're joking Lillian," I said. "We're not murderers. Or, at least two out of three people in this room aren't murderers. Lilies. Clever. Looks like you didn't mind how Aunt Inez suffered for weeks while her organs slowly shut down and no one knew why."

My sentence caught in my throat. To think my beloved aunt had suffered so much because of greed. I thought I might choke to death on my own sadness.

I owed it to Aunt Inez to get the truth.

"You have no proof," she said. "You know nothing. You were going to give the ring away! After all the work I've done to find all three."

"Oh, you have all three?"

She gritted her teeth. Was she going to growl? "I haven't done anything. Inez was sick. I cared for her. Reese died by accident. I don't even have any rings in my possession, so you don't have anything on me."

I could see she believed her own argument. Her shoulders relaxed slightly. She stood taller. Her chin jutted out.

"You admit you know your sister is dead?" Stormy was standing in the living room now, looking like she owned it.

Lillian didn't move. Her eyes darted back and forth between us.

"I think you're forgetting," I said. "You hired an assassin to murder me and Stormy."

"Lies," she said. "Fitzwilliam found out about the rings and the map and worked alone. I had nothing to do with it."

"Not true," a calm voice said behind me.

"Cecily has entered the chat," Stormy said, stifling an inappropriately timed laugh.

Lillian could barely squeeze out her words. "Cecily."

"I know everything, Aunt Lillian."

"Everything?" Lillian asked.

"Yes, everything. All about Ravenous Partners. The murders. The treasure."

"We wanted you to have it all! The whole treasure. Cecily, we were trying to get the rings from these two so you could be taken care of."

"You thought my parents had the rings and, therefore, the keys to the treasure. You and your Ravenous Partners had them killed. You didn't find them, so the killing continued. You won't stop until you've got your tiny, birdlike hands on all that money, wherever it is."

The silence was palpable.

What could Lillian possibly say?

I let the facts hang in the air like a toxic cloud.

"Do you have the map?" Lillian's voice trembled, but she was focused.

"The map?" Stormy was in a rage. "Did you not hear what you did to these women? Do you not have anything you want to say to them?"

Lillian crumpled to the floor.

"Can I …see it? See the map?"

"No, Gollum, you can't," Stormy said. "You need to get your priorities straight."

"So much work. So many lies. For nothing." Lillian began to weep.

"So, you admit it?" I asked. "You killed Aunt Inez? You hired Diving Bill Fitzwilliam to dispose of Stormy and me?"

Lillian wailed in anguish. From anyone else, it would have been an agonizing cry. From her, it sounded hollow, the screech of a person who'd been caught. Nothing more.

"I did all of it," she said, whimpering. "I poisoned the broth. Hired the assassin. I'm a villain."

"*I did all of it. I poisoned the broth. Hired the assassin. I'm a villain.*" Waggery had memorized her confession. And Stormy had recorded it.

"What a good—"

The door crashed open before I could finish telling Waggery what a good boy he was. Uniforms spilled through the entryway; lights flashed outside.

In the chaos, I heard Lillian scream, Stormy hoot, and Waggery caw. Afterwards, I found Waggery outside, resting on Titanic's shoulder. Stormy joined us next, took one look at Grist's devastated face, and began to cry. I cried. Titanic cried. Waggery said, "Boo-hoo-hoo."

"Where's Cecily?" I asked.

I searched the gathering crowd and found her at the edge, alone in her gray cloak.

I waved her over and wrapped my arms around her, pulling her into the group hug.

"I didn't want to intrude," she said through her sobs.

"Never," I said. "You're my Justice card."

§

I spent every night of our final summer with Aunt Inez, perched at the foot of her bed, reading to her, listening to her stories, or sitting quietly. I'd open her windows and let the cool, coastal breezes wash over us like a prayer. I was present for her then, determined to remember everything. The way her eyes crinkled when she laughed, and how she snorted when a joke was too funny.

I also bore witness to her compassion for others. Day after day, she continued to meet with her clients, sharing her revelations, helping them craft the stories of their lives. She never complained. Never uttered a snarky comment about anyone, even though I knew her well enough to know she could snark with the best of them.

One balmy evening, my favorite kind, we were reading together, when she looked up at me and said, "There's a wheel of life, Carrie."

I glanced up to see if she was making an odd joke. I couldn't think of a comeback, so I didn't say anything.

"Like the Wheel of Fortune card in tarot. To me, it's the most important card."

"Why?" I asked. "Out of all the cards like Death, Lovers, Justice—why would Wheel of Fortune be the most important? It doesn't have much of a meaning to me other than stuff happens."

"That's exactly why," she said, growing more animated. "It's a reminder. Life is a wheel, and it's always spinning through your experiences. The wheel features universal things. Love, friendship, career, finances, adventure, health, spirituality... round and round and round it goes, delivering these things to us, taking it all away. Bringing it back, but maybe only a little, then a lot. It's the card emblazoned with the secret name for the most powerful force in the universe. This card, the one telling us we have the least control, is the card we need to which we must pay the most attention."

"I'm not sure I get it," I said.

"You're young," she said. "When you reach my age, you'll understand wisdom comes from our fortunes made and lost. Remember to always be your own center. Whether you're rich or poor, have career failures or successes, lose people, find them again, have a genetic family or a found family. Hold yourself steady. Hold yourself accountable. Be ready for surprises you want and surprises you don't. Always, always run toward love, even if it comes wrapped in a tricky package. And know, Carrie, that you are loved in return."

§

Chapter Forty-Six

The aftermath of my journey to Mariner's Cove was equal parts joyous and bleak. Stormy, Cecily, and I had the three rings and the map. We had each other. Grist was heartbroken and needed time to heal. So did I.

We each returned to Prosperity for a while. Grist wanted to get back to work as quickly as possible. I needed to be in my own cottage to process my grief. Stormy and I spoke every day, but Grist kept his distance.

I couldn't let silence grow between us. He was my family.

After several days of not hearing from him, I did a little kidnapping of my own.

"Get in the car, we're going to Mariner's Cove," I said, grabbing his keys out of the bowl he kept by his cottage's front door.

"I can't," he said. "Carrie. My life is... I can't do it. I can't ever go back there."

"You have no choice," I said. "Tonight, the new and improved Ravenous Partners—me, Stormy, Cecily, Titanic, you, and a whole buncha pirates—are going to plan our expedition to Beryl Bay to uncover a treasure. LeMarcus is coming, and he's your favorite. I can't think of a more Grist-like thing than what we're about to do. Get in."

After much hemming and hawing, he agreed, and we were off. Waggery snoozed in his crate and seemed to be feeling fine when we arrived.

We arrived at Stormy's to find food, music, pirates, and rum. Grist, much to my relief, got into the swing of things right away, swapping stories with Titanic and making plans to offer guided docent tours of The Shipwrecks to earn more money for their upkeep. He and LeMarcus made each other laugh. Grist was an extrovert, after all. He needed people around him for energy. I was determined to keep him busy and surrounded by people who loved him.

Stormy and I were on solid footing again after deep discussions, promises to no longer kidnap people, and to always keep our phones charged. I knew she was the kind of person who needed a touch of danger in her life and if she wanted a tiny secret, I'd allow it. She'd always come through in her own diabolical way.

I think.

"Ok, enough!" Stormy called. "Those of you who aren't Ravenous Partners need to get out. We've got work to do and we don't want to be distracted by the likes of you."

"Am I Ravenous Partners?" Seaweed McGee asked.

"If you have to ask, you are not," Stormy said.

Scurvy Doug approached me. "Hey, Carrie. I wanted to thank you. For everything."

"Truth be told, Doug, I didn't do much."

"You were a friend when I needed it most. And I don't know what you guys are doing here, but I'd like to be a part of it. No need to pay me or anything. I want to help."

I'd had a hot buttered rum and was feeling generous. "Of course, Doug. Stay. You're going to love it."

I was excited to begin this phase of my life. So much darkness and sadness had surrounded me. Embarking on an adventure with the love of my life and my new friends felt like the best way to begin healing.

I hoped that Cecily and I would eventually become close. I knew it was going to be a slow process because we were both so deep in grief. But we were kind to each other, curious, helpful—even if we were still trying to figure out how to build a relationship.

She hadn't arrived yet. "Where's Cecily?" I asked Stormy.

"Something about picking up a package. She's running late, but she'll be here. We can start without her."

So, I did.

"Thank you all for joining the Ravenous Partners round table," I said. I looked into everyone's eyes and my heart surged with love and belonging. "I've added Scurvy Doug to our ranks, as he has proven himself brave and worthy. Are there any objections?"

None.

"Let's get started. This project comes down to the planning. We may not be the only people on the hunt for treasure—"

"Treasure?" Scurvy Doug whispered. Grist gave him a wink.

"—so, I think the best move is to pre-plan as much as possible and get out at lightning speed. Plus, we need to swear to each other now that we're going to keep this secret. It's got to stay between us." I knew keeping a secret like this in a group this large would be next to impossible, but it was worth a try.

"I'm so honored," Scurvy Doug said. He started to cry. "You trust me."

"Can you trust me?"

The voice came from the darkened doorway. It was Cecily.

Everyone turned to see who spoke.

"I have some news," she said. Her face was as gray as her cloak.

Titanic stood up. "Are you alright, lass? Have a seat. Doug, get Cecily some water."

"What's happening?" I asked in Stormy's general direction. She shrugged.

Cecily placed a letter-sized envelope on the table in front of her. Her ring sparkled in the light. I looked at mine and at Stormy's and felt kinship.

"Since the events of the past few weeks, I've been doing a deep dive into the circumstances surrounding Ravenous Partners and the death of my parents."

The silence was thick. Everyone leaned in.

"I thought I'd learned their real names, so I found police reports, news articles. Anything I could get my hands on about their death. I uncovered some difficult truths. I also discovered some strange and wondrous developments. Before I shared them with you all, I needed proof."

No one spoke. Cecily didn't look anyone in the eye.

"In this folder, I have a DNA test. Standard online thing, the kind where you send them a swab. It arrived an hour ago."

Waggery hopped up and down on his perch. "Cecily," he said. "Cecily. Cecily. Cecily. Mwah!"

"Shh. Not now, Wags," I said. "Go on. What did you learn?"

Cecily stood up and turned her back to the room, as if she was steeling herself for what came next. She turned back. Her eyes were filled with tears.

"It's about Carrie."

Stormy was up now. "What? What's wrong with Carrie?"

"Nothing's wrong with Carrie," Cecily said. "She's my sister."

END

About the Author

Bethany Browning is the BIBA-winning author of **Sasquatch, Baby!** (which was also short-listed for the North Street Book Prize), **Dead Spread**, **Queen of Tentacles, Shimmerfish**, and **Men Going Mad**, and is co-writer of the feature film **War of the Wills (2023)**. Her fiction has appeared in several online publications and print anthologies. Her story **Charred Cedar** was nominated for Sundress Publications' 2022 Best of the Net, and **How I Cured My Depression** was nominated for the same award, as well as for a place in the Best Mystery Stories anthology in 2023. She writes short stories, cozy mysteries, horror, humor, and any other genre that piques her interest. She is a member of the Horror Writers Association and Sisters in Crime.

Follow her on Threads @bethanybrowningbooks or contact her directly at bethany@bethanybrowning.com. Her website is bethanybrowning.com.

www.ingramcontent.com/pod-product-compliance
Lightning Source LLC
Chambersburg PA
CBHW070453300726

48975CB00007B/2160